**Armageddon,
Texas**

Also by Tommy Zurhellen

Nazareth, North Dakota
(Book 1 of The Messiah Trilogy)

Apostle Islands
(Book 2 of The Messiah Trilogy)

**Armageddon,
Texas**   *a novel*

TOMMY ZURHELLEN

An Atticus Trade Paperback Original

ATTICUS
BOOKS

20 Waverly Place, 2nd Floor
Madison, NJ 07940
http://atticusbooksonline.com

ISBN-13: 978-0-9915469-1-6
ISBN-10: 0-99915469-1-1

Typeset in Fairfield by David McNamara
Cover design by Jamie Keenan

Acknowledgments

Three cheers to Dan Cafaro at Atticus Books for all his hard work, patience and unwavering support in championing this trilogy, from start to finish. Also, thanks and congratulations to artist Jamie Keenan, for completing a rare trifecta of amazing book covers. *Slainte!*

The third time's the charm to express my gratitude to Gary Clark and the Vermont Studio Center for granting me a third residency to complete parts of this book. Thanks also to Marist College, especially its President, Dr. Dennis J. Murray, for so much ongoing support and encouragement on this trilogy. Thanks to Fabrizio & Carla at La Scuola Lorenzo de' Medici in Firenze, for the gracious use of their space and resources as I wrote and researched parts of this book in Italy. *Salute!*

Special thanks to my invaluable third watch of readers, Emily Vizzo and Baker Lawley, who always respond to my three-alarm fires with buckets of insight and kindness. Thanks also to Nicole Hardy for the gift that gave this book its third eye. Thanks to all my friends and colleagues for their encouragement along the way, especially Heather M. Finck, Suzanne Morrison, Hyeseung Marriage-Song, Ed Smith, Jody Gehrman, Mara Pagliai, Vanessa & John, Dayna Grundland, Josh Galitsky, Chris Pryslopski, and all the

VSC crew, especially Chris Motta, Yassin Adnan and Karen Geiger; thanks to Zoran Poposki for the golden dragon, and to Erika Adams, for that French. *A votre sante!*

Finally, thanks to the original Sassy McSasserton, for being the first to hear the whole idea for this book over lunch, and for not laughing out loud into her three-bean salad.

for fireball—
crooked mouth, crooked HEART

Contents

...The fire-serpent—
terrible, horror-spattered—was scorched with flames.
He was fifty foot-spans long as he lay. Once he had reveled
in sky-soaring at night and swooping back down to his cave. Death-stiff,
he would get no more joy from earth-caves.
Near him remained
cups and pitchers, plates and noble swords.
They were all rusty,
bearing the embrace of earth from a thousand winters.
That legacy in all its vastness—bygone people's gold—
had been wound round with a spell so that no man could enter that
ring-hall unless God himself, triumphant truth-king, protector of man,
had entrusted the desired one to open the hoard—only the one man
who seemed most fitting to him.

—*Beowulf* LINES 3040-57
(TRANSLATION FROM OLD ENGLISH BY MOIRA FITZGIBBONS)

Dance, Mary Magdalene; dance, dance and sing,
For unto you is born
This day a King.

—W.R. RODGERS

Earth Without Form, and Void

If you're reading this now, I guess that means this old witch is already dead. Ding dong. And about time, I say: I feel my memory fading down to the last cobweb and I don't have time for history lessons—wait, wait, here's something I remember! There was an old song that went *don't know much about history, don't know much geology*—or something like that. *Science books, big French cooks.* Anyway, history was in there somewhere.

If you are reading this now, you've probably got a lot of questions. Truth is, I was never the kind of girl to hold onto anything too long, especially answers. But I can tell you what I remember. If you're reading this, you're probably looking around and shaking your head, saying goddamn, how in holy Hell did this world fall apart so fast? And truth is, so am I.

I remember there was a war. I don't know who won. I just

know we lost. *What a wonderful world this would be.* That was in there, too. *Slide rule at four.*

I realize a song don't help your questions much.

But I do remember it was a good fucking song.

Sure, I remember the end of the world. It started on a Wednesday night.

What I remember is waking up in the dark to check on the baby. We were living outside Florence then, just me and the boy, on a hill overlooking the city; it must have been winter, because I remember my cold toes sliding across the red tile and my fingers wiping the white frost that framed the windows. The house was silent, and the only light came from the kitchen: at night, I'd leave the little TV on with no sound, usually the BBC News, so I could pretend there was someone to talk to while I stared out the window and waited for him to come back for us. And I remember walking back through the kitchen that night to shut the damn thing off, but instead I had to cover my mouth because I saw the caption they had scrolling across the screen: DRAGON BURNS DALLAS TEXAS TO THE GROUND. I remember that video looping over and over, thirty seconds of an entire city flooded by fire like a goddamn monster movie. Hell, it *was* a monster movie, a fucking marathon I watched for hours and still didn't believe was real. And I wish I could tell you the first words out of my mouth that night were something important, you know, something Winston Churchill or one of those old Greek guys in togas might have said. But no. The first thing I said was, "fucking *Laz*," because for once in his sorry life my brother had told the truth: the end of the world would come with dragons. And then I remember looking around the house for the good bourbon and something big to pour it in because I wanted to celebrate. I remember sitting there and being happy for the last time in my life while I watched a city burn to the ground. All I could think was, *it won't be long now*. And do you believe I actually packed a bag and woke the baby to wrap him in a blanket, like there was going to be a limo or a helicopter showing up any moment? Stupid girl. I remember dancing across that fucking kitchen floor like a ballerina with a sippy cup of bourbon in my hand while the whole world died. I remember laughing. I was thinking, *it won't be long until he comes back for me*.

That was thirty years ago.

If you are reading this now, I already know what you're thinking: who the hell was Winston Churchill? What day was Wednesday? Why can't I find Florence or Texas or China or dragons on any map? And now suddenly I realize, shit—if you're reading this and you can't understand English, then nothing I say matters anyway. Truth is, I thought about drawing all this out in pictures instead, like those cave paintings of deers and wooly mammoths on the wall, but with my withered hands I'd draw even worse than I write so if you put a knife to my throat and told me to draw a fire-breathing dragon it'd probably come out looking like a drunk caterpillar or a dandelion, and who does that help? I can only imagine the people in the next world—your world—looking at my drawings like they mean something important, and for the next million years folks believe the last world was destroyed by evil flowers and bugs.

Truth is, you can't find Florence because it's underwater now. Ding dong. And I don't really remember who Winston Churchill was, either. And I can't really tell you if sabre tooth tigers and wooly mammoths were real or not, because they came a little before my time—but *dragons*, well, I certainly saw my share. Rumor is, there's one still living in a mountain somewhere in Texas. That's what people used to call the desert on the other side of the Alabama Sea. That's where me and the boy are headed.

Wait I remember something else! *All my exes live in Texas.* Truth is, that's where the whole war started.

I named my son Sam, after the father. I know it's been thirty years since he was born because I would count the days to make sure the kid had a birthday every year. After the war, the handful of folks left behind stopped keeping track of things like time, but we found ways to get by. Once in a while we'd pass by someone going the other way and trade whatever we had. When people see my son, they call him a freak. They take one look at his size and that ugly scar across his face and call him a Monster—imagine that, in a world where you got real live monsters running around, eating people. But I just call him special. I call him my son. I love him. You're going to think this is silly, but to me, he is the closest thing we have to God. He's probably the only reason I've made it this far. And besides, less and less folks seem to be around to make fun, anyway. Old age, I guess. And dragons. Ding dong.

If you're reading this, I'm curious. What kind of Gods do you have?

We had some doozies. But what I remember about my Sam are the good times.

But that was a long time ago.

If you are reading this now, I really wish there was some-place you could go and learn about all the mistakes we made back then—the Titanic, the Bay of Pigs, the oil spills, the civil wars, the atom bombs, the Doobie Brothers—but far as I know all that's sitting at the bottom of the ocean now, or covered in giant mudslides, or just plain old de-stroyed, burned right to the ground.

I think I already mentioned the fire-breathing dragons.

The world looks so different now. Did you know Ant-arctica used to be covered in snow? The whole thing! And did you know we had a whole bunch of different places on the planet called North Pole? Did you know we had giant airplanes flying all over the world that served little cups of orange juice and wine, and paper slippers for your feet? And did you know we invented pajamas with socks already sewed into them so your feet didn't get cold?

What do you call Antarctica now? Do you have polar bears and penguins? Do they have to live in Africa and Australia?

Look at me. Now I'm the one with all the questions.

Listen, if you find this and no one can read it, just remember one word: DAYLENE HOOKER. Shit that's two words. Ding dong. But say it anyway. Again. With a little gusto. That's it. Gusto was an Italian word that meant, *gusto.* I used to live there. Italy, not gusto. Before Italy, I remember I lived in France. Now they're both gone. I heard you can still see a little bit of the Eiffel Tower sticking out of the water.

Don't know much about Pough-keep-sie. No, that's just wrong.

But Daylene Hooker, that was right. That was my name! That was me.

I.
Light From the Darkness

When this was Texas, everyone would ride around in transportations called pickup trucks and wear unusual hats and drink the urine of farm animals. (Urine is an old English word for *piss*.) In Texas, there were many boys and girls my size with strange names like Nerd and Douchebag and Kevin. They would all go to the Prison located in their city to read books and learn how to make sex. (Sex is another old word that means *poontang*, but in Texas if you stated "poontang" out loud, old people would hit you or put you in a room with a bed, until you starved to death.) Accordion to Hyatt, who is old, boys were not allowed to state many French words, either, like *fucknuts* or *dingleberry*. Hyatt states girls were allowed to use French words, but only when they made sex. Hyatt is a wizard, which is English for being *lazy* or a *liar*. In Texas, there were special days called Friday and Saturday when larger boys would

drive pickup trucks to their Prison and dress up in cos-
tumes to fight in a tournament called Football while old
people watched the Football and drank more urine out of
metal barrels and cans. When a boy would become injured
in the fighting he was carried away so he could die alone.
Then after the Football, the girls of Texas would make sex
with the boys in their pickup trucks.

I have never observed a real pickup truck.

To be honest, I have never observed a real girl, either.

I am told there was once a girl in Armageddon, but she
was only here for one day and she is now in Disneyland.
Disneyland is how you used to say Hell. The girl was named
Lily. She was shoplifted by the Dragon into the mountain
and probably eaten. In the old world, Lily was another way
to say *flower.* I am told she was very beautiful. I am told she
was missing some parts, too, just like me.

The old people of Armageddon call me Kid. This is not
a proper name, like Lily or Herodotus or Big Dick McGee,
because in English *kid* simply meant small child or young
goat. To be honest, I do like to climb rocks like a goat when
it is daylight, but if I was a boy in the old world I would possess at least three or four names, like all the other Prison
boys and girls. In Texas, you had to remember a fuck-ton
of names. (Fuck-ton is French for *a lot.*) A boy had a first
name, a last name, a middle name, a nick-name, a pet name
if your job was to be someone's pet, and perhaps a code
name if you were a superhero. (A nick-name was the name
your enemies gave you, which was different than the name

Nick.) In the old world, your names came from either a mother or a father, or sometimes both, and they had to give you many names because at the End there were more than seven billion persons living in Texas, and a billion was one thousand millions in a row, which is certainly a fuck-ton.

In Texas, having more than one name was important. Example: there once was a man named John Jacob Astor, but another man had to be named John Jacob Jingleheimer Schmidt so other persons could tell them apart. Sometimes when the people of Texas became lazy and took names for granite, they would only pronounce your initials. Examples: J.J for John Jacob, or B.D. for Big Dick. (Dick was another way to say *Richard*.) Here in Armageddon, Hyatt, who is lazy, calls everyone "a dirty S.O.B." which accordion to Ben stands for Stick Of Butter. I have observed sticks of butter in the picture books of Carnegie, but they were never dirty. They were cold bricks the color of toenails. In the storybooks, the boys and girls of Texas would sit at a table and rub butter on their food while the mothers and fathers watched. Then the boys and girls took transportations to the local Prison. This was called a *family*. Sometimes there was a pie sitting on a windowsill. If the window was open, the pie was usually shoplifted by birds or dogs or evil wizards, when the family was not looking.

Sometimes Hyatt calls me the initials A.D.H.D. but I do not know what this stands for.

This could be my code name, since I am told I am also an Alien. (Alien is English for *special*.) I know I am special because I am missing some body parts, and because I possess a superpower. Hyatt often states to me, "You got a few screws loose, Kid." But this is silly because I am not a robot, I am a boy.

It is true, I am a very Alien boy.

I live in the basement of Carnegie with all the books. We are lucky to possess one working Doo-Hickey remaining at Carnegie, and at night when Ben and Hyatt sit in chairs and take their medicine they let me choose the records to put on it. (Record is another word for *history*.) The basement of Carnegie where I sleep has shelves with many histories but Hyatt only likes to listen to sad people play guitar and sing like they are choking on food. Example: there is a record called "All My Ex's Live in Texas" that I like because it is very funny. (In Texas, an Ex was a woman who refused to poontang you, because she was angry at something you did previously.) This history is about a man in Texas named George Strait who made a lot of women angry. He was running from women, who all possess names that rhyme with the old cities of Texas: Abilene, Galveston, Texarkana. He does not say the name of a girl here in Armageddon, but I think it would be hard to find a name that rhymes with Armageddon. The women of Texas become so angry at George Strait he must live far away in a place called Tennessee, which was over four hundred miles north of Texas. (A mile was 5,280 small steps in the same direction.) Ben states no one lives there anymore. I know no one lives in Abilene, Galveston or Texarkana either because now they are all under the Alabama Sea. I am guessing fish live there now. And sea monsters.

Hyatt calls these records about angry women and transportations and urine *Country*. Ben states they are called crap, which was the same as *shit*, an old French word that means human feces. Ben likes a different type of history called Heavy Metal, but there is presently no Heavy Metal in the basement of Carnegie. We do possess a record about a metal robot from the island of Japan who is named Mister Roboto, but Ben often states this is definitely *not* Heavy Metal. But I like to play it and dance like a robot when no one is looking, except for Dog, who is a dog and also likes to dance, but like a dog robot.

At the End, most people of Texas spoke in English, and before English, the people of Texas all spoke Spanish, which was brought by metal robots called the Conquistadores. Before that everyone would speak Roman and Greek, like Herodotus, who was the first historian of Texas. A historian was a special person who told stories that were true, which was the opposite of a wizard. Herodotus is my hero because we are both historians and we both like to make lists. He only needed one name and it already started with Hero. He wrote about dragons, too, just like me. I am the first historian of the New World and that is why I write down lists of everything I see and hear. Example:

LIST OF FRENCH WORDS HYATT USES MOST FREQUENTLY.

1. "Shit!"
2. "Dipshit!"
3. This is a tie between: "Dick-tard!" and "Fuck-ton." (A tie is when you cannot decide.)
4. "Motherfucker!" Example: "Waking up this morning was a motherfucker!"
5. "Dipshit motherfucker!"

My best friend in Armageddon is named Dog. He is a dog. The old persons of Armageddon named him Dog before I came here. In Texas, a dog was a small wolf that could tolerate humans without eating them. Dog is the only dog of Armageddon, just as I am the only kid. When we are not working, we solve mysteries. Dog does not like the pretending part of being a detective, because pretending is a kind of lie and as a rule dogs do not lie, but we possess no choice because there is no Prison or Football or pickup trucks in Armageddon. Dog tells me that dogs only deal in Facts, which is good when you are detecting a mystery. Example: my job every morning is to count the number of alive animals and also the number of alive persons inside the wall. Yesterday the number I wrote down in my book for alive persons totally was twenty-seven. Two days ago the number was twenty-nine, but yesterday "Sassy McSasserton" died because she was very old. (I am putting her name into quotation marks because I do not believe that was her real name.)

And three days ago, the body of the old hero named Big Dick McGee was found outside the wall. He was certainly eaten by something. Question: what was Big Dick doing outside the wall after darkness? Dog and I cannot answer this Question.

When you cannot answer the Question, this is called a mystery.

Hyatt states, "Sounds like a job for Kid and Dog. The world's first detectives."

Hyatt likes to call me the first *everything*, because I am the only human in Armageddon who is not old. Example: when I go out to the rocks and dig for dragon bones, he states I am the first archaeologist. When I draw my maps of the New World, he states I am the first mapmaker. When I go outside the walls in the daylight, I am the first explorer and when I come back before sunset, I am the first Prodigal Son. (He does not know this, but I will be the first person to swim across the Gihon River without being eaten. Dog will be the first dog. We will swim it together. We are not supposed to do this alone.)

And when I am old enough, I will become the first Dragonslayer, too.

When this was Texas, there were Dragons everywhere. In Armageddon we only have the one who sleeps inside the mountain, but previously, the world was filled with all kinds of Dragons and they had strange names, too, like Brontosaurus, alligator, Bruce Lee and Puff. Accordion to a history we have in Carnegie by three people named Peter, Paul and Mary, Puff was a magic dragon that lived by the sea. Hyatt states that Puff is only a metaphor about smoking weeds. (Metaphor is another word for *lie*.) I do not believe him because we have listened to the history of Puff on Fisher Price many times and there is no mention of smoking weeds and besides, Hyatt is a known wizard, which means he has the power to help people by inventing things, but it also means he is a liar.

He states, "It's the same with Lucy in the Sky with the Fucking Diamonds, Kid."

I do not know this Lucy, but I know enough about Texas from my books to observe Dragons were real.

There are many words from the old world I do not understand. Examples: shindig, cahoots, cornucopia, nerd, labradoodle, love. The worst of these is love. In Texas, the word love could mean almost anything: you could love a mother or father, a boy or girl, a dog, a farm animal, a food item, even a transportation. Love could even mean *hate*, the opposite of love. This makes no sense; people could state, "I love you" to other persons who wanted to murder or shoplift them, like an Ex or a Demon. Many of the books in the basement of Carnegie use this word, over and over again. Example: there is a history called *One Night With a Cowboy* where a woman called Lady Margarita states to the Cowboy who is named Randy Hunt, "It is impossible for me to love a man like you, Randy." But on the very next page, she poontangs him. To be honest, I am confused. Was she lying? If she was lying, did Randy Hunt know it was a lie? Later, when they are alone at someplace called the prairie, Randy

Hunt states, "I love that blue Ford F-150 almost as much as I love you, Margarita." Ford F-150 was another name for a pickup truck, which even a boy knows cannot not love you in return.

What did love really mean? If a word was used so often, how much could it be worth? To me, love is the most confusing word in all of Texas because every time I ask myself a Question about it, the answer is always more Questions.

Hyatt would state, this is another mystery for Kid and Dog.

Question: in Texas, when people stated, "I love you," how many times was this a lie?

At night, I wake up when I hear the screams outside the wall. They pierce the walls of Carnegie and make my neck shiver even though I sleep deep in in the basement, protected by many stacks of books. Tonight it sounds like an old woman's voice and it states: *Oh God, please help me. Don't let me die out here.* The voice is crying like it has lost a child. *Oh God, please let me in.* (I am not putting these voices into quotations like the books in Carnegie, because quotation marks were only used for humans speaking words out loud, and these voices outside the wall are not human.) They sound like alive persons, but they are really monsters, which is an old word for Demon. Sometimes the voice is a man, or sometimes a small boy or girl. Once it was the voice of a dog, but only Dog and I could understand what it was trying to say. Sometimes the voices outside the wall even call you by name. But they are all monsters who just want to eat you. Hyatt states that monsters are the evil creatures left over from the War who did not return home to Disneyland, like the crawling ones Hyatt named Lawyers and the flying ones he named Telemarketers.

And of course, there is a dragon who lives in our mountain. We call it Dragon.

Tonight Hyatt, Ben and Dog and I are sitting on the flat roof of Carnegie. We all cannot sleep so we are playing cards while the voices are whales in the dark. Hyatt is shuffling the playing cards when he states, "What's it going to be, dipshits? What do you motherfuckers want to lose at tonight? Pardon my French, Kid." Hyatt has taught me all the authentic card games of Texas: Reverse Cowgirl, Two Rats in a Sack, Bank Foreclosure and something named Panty Raid. (Authentic means not a lie.) I have never won at card games with Hyatt but he states, "As long as you keep bringing food to bet with, you'll keep improving."

Dog does not play cards, but he likes to sit beside me and observe the cards in my hand, which for some reason are also called a hand. Tonight I am using an old strategy on Ben that Hyatt has taught me. It is called *cheating*. Example: whenever Ben turns his head to look at the wall to make sure nothing is trying to crawl over the Barbara wire, I slip another card off the stack of cards, which is called a deck. Every time I use cheating, Dog states to me, "If I were you, I would not do that." (Luckily, a dog can never be a boy.) Even more luckily, I am the only person in Armageddon who can understand Dog when he talks, which is a good superpower to possess if you have to cheat in front of a dog.

This is my superpower: I can converse with all the farm animals, too, except the mule, but that is not my fault because he does not like talk to anyone except himself. His name is Gus, which in Texas meant *gloomy*. He is definitely gloomy.

Hyatt shuffles the deck again and states, "How about an old-fashioned game of Absentee Landlord? I'll deal." Ben grumbles, because Hyatt is a wizard and he likes to invent things, especially card games. But Ben and Hyatt are best friends, just as Dog and I are best friends. When Ben goes on his adventures, Hyatt stays behind in Armageddon to invent all the things Ben needs on his adventures, like TNT, which means explosives. Sometimes Hyatt works all day in his workshop, pouring one cup into another cup. This is called *science*.

The whales outside the wall grow louder, and I feel my neck get cold again. This voice is stating, *God have mercy. Don't leave me out here in the wilderness to die, Kid. Please help me.*

Dog sees me shiver. "Don't be afraid. It'll be light out soon."

"I am not afraid." Dog knows I do not like to lie, but I do not want Ben to observe my fear, either, because he is a superhero and is always brave. I state loudly, "They are just like the Sirens. In the Odyssey of Homer."

Hyatt shakes his head behind his cards. "You sure read a lot of fucking books, Kid."

I state in response, "I live in a library. I do not possess much choice."

Ben smiles to me and states, "Good point, Kid."

Ben is what people in Texas called a superhero. This means he is worth at least three or four normal heroes. Example: Big Dick McGee, who followed Ben on many adventures before he was eaten outside the wall, was a normal hero. He did heroic deeds but did not have superpowers like Ben. When this was Texas, anyone could be a hero, but to be a superhero you had to do things other people could not do, like magic. (Hyatt states he can do magic but I know this is fake.) In the basement of Carnegie there are stories of many super heroes with unusual names like Batman and Catwoman and Bill Cosby, but accordion to Hyatt, Ben is the only one left. Before the War, his whole name was Benjamin Owen Wolf.

LIST OF SUPERHERO DEEDS OF BENJAMIN OWEN WOLF

1. Swam across the entire Bay of Oklahoma, without being eaten.

2. Slept outside the wall of Armageddon at night, without being eaten.

3. Fought a dragon during the War, without being eaten.

4. Killed the outlaw Frank Dayraven in the Holy Land.

5. T.B.D. (these are initials which mean To Be Deter-

mined, which means this deed will happen later, at which point I will cross out ~~T.B.D.~~ and replace it with the heroic deed.)

T.B.D. will probably be replaced when Ben crosses the Alabama Sea, which is why he is preparing the boats for tomorrow. This is the job of a historian: when Ben returns he will tell me the stories of all his adventures and I will write them down, just as Herodotus did for the superheroes of old Texas. Ben will tell me more about the world, and I will add this to my maps. The book *People and Nations* states, to have history there must be persons performing great deeds, and there must be other persons to write the deeds down.

The voices are not going away. *I am going to die out here alone if you do not help me.*

Ben must be observing my fear because he states, "Reading's a good thing, Kid. I guess I used to read a lot of books, too, when I was your age. Before I got into other stuff."

"Yeah," Hyatt states. "Like girls." Dog's ears go up, because he is interested in girls.

I will die if you do not come to save me. Please, please, I am begging you. Please.

Ben is ignoring the voice outside the wall. "Yeah, sure, girls, music, football. Then I joined the Navy, and that all went away." He smiles, like he is holding a memory inside his head. "Then I got married, and it *really* all went away."

I want to ask Ben so many more Questions, about the girls of Texas and football and pickup trucks and his Ex, but I do not want to be a pest. (Sometimes when I ask the old people too many Questions they call me a pest, which is another word for *insect*.) But if I am going to be the first historian, I know I must learn to ask Questions.

So I turn over a new page in my notebook and I state to Ben, "Why did you get married?"

Ben does not state anything in response right away. He rubs his shoulder as if there is a wound there, but I know there is not. "It's just what you did. It was a crazy world, Kid. You got a job, you met someone you didn't absolutely hate, and then after a few months you asked them to marry you."

I write all this down. "Hyatt often states he never was married."

"Yeah, well, look up *outlaw* in that big dictionary of yours in the basement, and you'll see a picture of old Hyatt here."

I state, "But this is a lie. I have looked up this word before when you told me the story of the killing of Frank Dayraven, and there is no picture of anyone there."

He laughs. "It's just an expression, Kid."

It is odd to hear Ben, who is a superhero, tell a lie. I find my list of the English words that translate to lies and add *expression*.

LIST OF ENGLISH WORDS THAT TRANSLATE TO LIES.
1. Trick
2. Tale

3. Joke or Joking
4. Sarcasm
5. Fantasy
6. Metaphor or Poem (same)
7. Fish
8. Pretend
9. Expression

(I do not observe why fish means lie, but in Texas it seems if you told a story about a fish to someone, it was automatically considered a lie.)

Ben observes me writing and states, "You really have an obsession with what's true, and what's not, don't you?"

I state exactly what Herodotus would have stated, which is, "Historians must deal in facts."

Ben laughs again. "Okay, Kid, okay. I'll try to be more heroic around here, and give you something to write about. Where are you up to in that history book of yours, anyway?"

"The Conquistadores of Spain have just brought horses and smallpox to Texas."

"Good man. Keep going, there's a lot of good stuff coming up. I remember the French Revolution getting pretty gritty. Then there was the Alamo of course—not too far from here, as a matter of fact. And when you get to the Civil War, let me know." I nod my head and write down *Civil War*, which sounds like a very silly name for a war. Each war of Texas possessed its own name, which makes no sense, because to me all wars seem the same.

I state, "Tell me more about the War." When you state "the War" in Armageddon, the old people automatically know which war this is. Ben observes me for a moment and opens and closes his mouth a few times, but he does not state anything. I realize I am probably acting like an insect right now. Finally he states, "You'll have plenty of war stories of your own to tell, around this place."

But I want to know more. I want to know everything. "Tell me about your life as a boy in Prison, and about riding around with girls in pickup trucks, then."

"Now, that's a subject that'll take a lot of time to get right." Ben lays down his cards. This is a signal that he is finished playing the card game. "And it'll be dawn soon. You'd better go back down and try to get a little sleep, Kid."

I state, "One last Question." Ben nods, and I turn to my list of Questions about Texas, which is the longest list I possess in my notebook. "In Texas, what was a Reverse Cowgirl?"

Ben coughs suddenly. "Where did you learn that?"

I look up and state, "Hyatt." Beside me, Dog is laughing in his dog laugh, but I do not know why.

Ben turns to look at Hyatt, then states to me, "Well, um, you know what a cowboy was, right?" He has both hands over his face, which in Texas was the way you showed other people you did not want to state the words you were about to state out loud.

"Of course," I state. "Cowboys rode horses where the deer and the antelope play."

"That's right. So, um, a cowgirl was the same thing, but instead of a boy it was a girl. And a *reverse* cowgirl, well— she just rode her horse backwards, so she could see where she was coming from. Or if someone was sneaking up on her. Okay, there you have it, Reverse Cowgirl. Now, time for bed."

I stop writing and observe him. I state, "This makes no sense."

Hyatt looks at his arm and states, "Well, look at the time." He does this often, even though there is nothing on his arm but scars and hair. This is already on my list of Questions about Texas because I want to know how Hyatt is able to observe time by simply looking at his arm. Hyatt puts down his cards now, too, and slowly stands up and stretches his old legs. "We got a cubic butt-ton of work to do in the morning. Superhero Ben here is skipping out on us again, Kid, and we need to bury ol' B.D. and Sassy down by the river. So, Big fucking Day ahead. Pardon my French."

When Hyatt states the day will be big he is not referring to the size or length of the day, which is always the same because of the Sun. (This is more science.) Instead he is stating that tomorrow will be *important*, which I observe is actually not a lie because Ben is sailing east on another adventure. He will be gone for a long time. Some words in English like big can mean more than one thing, which I do not like because that means any word can lie. Accordion to Hyatt, French words are notorious for having many meanings. Example: shit. In the old world, you could state, "This food item is good *shit*" which meant the food item was especially good, but you could also state, "This food item is *shitty*" which meant it was especially bad.

To be honesty this is confusing; how did Herodotus manage to write down the truth in his books with all this confusion? How did he learn to separate the truth from all the lies persons like to tell?

O f all the ways people told lies in Texas, poetry was the most dangerous because everything in a poem pretended it was something else. The purpose of a poem was to trick you; it might describe a river or a tree but by the end you observe the poem was really about love, or pain, or death. A poem was automatically a lie because it asked Questions that possess no answers. There is a thick book in the basement of Carnegie filled with nothing but English poems. It has many poems that talk about love, but they are not about love, they are really about pain. There are poems that talk about pain, but they are really about love. And there are poems that talk about death, but they are really about love and pain. This makes no sense.

I am observing all the poems of Texas were about love, or pain, or death.

Whenever there was a war in Texas, the poets were always the first to die. I have just reached the French part of *People and Nations*, and in the French Revolution, the poets were the first to be put in the guillotine, which was a French way of chopping your head off and sending you to

Disneyland.

I am glad there is no more poetry in the world.

I n the daytime, the town of Armageddon looks like this:

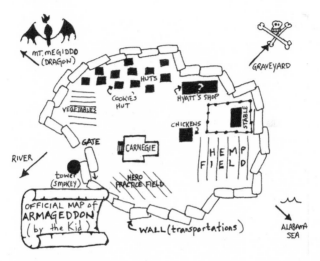

The wall around Armageddon is composed of old transportations and large rocks. Some of the transportations still possess authentic writing from the old world. Example: *Kansas City Southern Railway,* large yellow print. Kansas City was a place that was famous for its pretty women, accordion to a history by Fats Domino. Some of the writing on the transportations is not authentic. Example: *Kilroy Wuz Here,* loopy white script letters. I suspect this is a hairless lie because this writing appeared only twenty-three days ago. I have kept the history of alive persons in Armageddon for the previous eight hundred and sixteen days, and there has never been anyone here named Kilroy.

Possibility #1: a monster named Kilroy snuck over the wall. Evidence: monsters are probably bad spellers, and *wuz* is not a word. Possibility #2: an alive person named Yorlik wrote his name backwards, because it was dark or he was taking his medicine. But there are no alive persons in Armageddon named Yorlik, either.

Today the number of alive persons totally is twenty-eight, but I do not count myself because I am only a boy. I am also an Alien. I do not count the people who have floated down the river, either, because they have gone to Disneyland. When you become too old or sick, or you are eaten by something outside the wall, your spirit turns into a bird and you soar west over the mountains to Disneyland where Sam and his mother Roxy are waiting for you. This is what Ben states. He is a superhero and not a wizard, so I can believe him.

Ben states all the old people left after the War are going to Disneyland, even Hyatt.

Sometimes when Ben is out of range for hearing, Hyatt states, "You know, Kid, Sam will grant you three wishes, too," but this is another hairless lie. (Hyatt has no hair on his head, therefore it is easy to see when he is telling a lie.) Besides, I know Hyatt does not believe in Sam or Disneyland.

But just in case Hyatt is not lying, I have recorded my three wishes.

MY THREE WISHES WHEN I SEE SAM IN DISNEY-
LAND.

1. A pickup truck. Color: blue. Size: large, with room for
Bugs Meany in back.

2. A Prison where I can leave the truck so the girls can
speak French when they pass it.

3. A girl. No, a tattoo. (All the old people of Armageddon
possess tattoos. Ben has an anchor on his right arm and a
picture of Popeye on his left arm. Popeye was a super hero
from the old world who depended on canned foods for his
superpowers. I think my tattoos will all be of dragons.)

In the night time, Armageddon looks like this:

It is blank. Ha! It is blank because you cannot see anything in the dark. This is a *joke*. I do not normally like jokes because it seems you cannot tell a joke without telling a lie. Example: in Texas, it seems the funniest joke was to surprise someone by placing the peel of a banana on the floor and hoping they step on the peel and fall down. I do not understand why this is funny. Sometimes I try to make Dog laugh. It is very difficult to make a dog laugh, because dogs deal in Facts. In the books of Carnegie, whenever dogs laugh or become excited they state, "woof woof" or perhaps "ruff ruff." But when he laughs, Dog states, "Roo-AAA-rrrr—nn" which does not sound at all like woof or ruff. Perhaps he is an Alien, too, like me.

One day when we were out helping Hyatt collect rocks on the other side of the river for his wizard experiments, Dog slipped a fish into my trousers when I was not looking. Dog laughed all the way home in Hyatt's wagon, and even into the night. He howled "Roo-AAA-rrrr—nn" so loudly, all the farm animals of Armageddon laughed in their pens too, keeping everyone awake. Except the mule, who is gloomy and does not laugh.

Dog still laughs when he thinks of how he tricked me that day. For this situation, I have learned a new word in English: *Revenge*. But it is difficult to sneak up on a dog.

At dawn, Dog and I are outside the wall, busy detecting the mystery of Big Dick McGee. We agree the first thing to do is detect the place where Big Dick McGee's bones were found. Smokey is the hero in charge of open-ing and closing the gate in the daylight. When Dog and I wish to escape outside he states the same thing: "Don't get lost out there." But he must know this is silly because I am the first mapmaker, which means I make the maps, and as a rule the mapmaker cannot be lost. Painted on Smokey's metal watch tower are the words REMEMBER THE ALA-MO which comes from a part of *People and Nations* that I have not accomplished yet, although I am told there was a battle in Texas between the cowboys and the Conquistado-res, and the cowboys lost.

Smokey states, "All clear out there," which means he does not see any monsters left over from the darkness. He puts down his gun on the railing of the tower and leans over to us. "You two going out to the river again?"

"Perhaps. But we will be detecting a mystery first." Ac-cordion to Ben, we are allowed to go as far south as the river and as far west as the foot of the mountains. We are not allowed to travel in the direction called north, which is towards the battlefield. The old people call this the Graveyard. (Dog and I found a helmet once, rolling along with the desert wind. It had a hole in it. One day we came to the edge of the graveyard, where we also came across the tail of an airplane, sticking out of the ground. From afar, we could observe swarms of insects flying all around like a black cloud, but when we get closer we know these are not insects, but big black birds, twisting and turning in the hot air. When we get even closer we observe they are not birds, either, but something very, very different, something we will never find in any book in the basement of Carnegie.)

Smokey waves from his tower as we pass through the gate. "Well, you know the drill, Kid. Happy hunting. Look after that Kid, Dog."

Dog barks two short barks and one long bark, which can mean either "I understand you" or "caterpillar" in dog. (In this case, it means "I understand you.")

I look up at Smokey and state, "Sam be with you." I state this because Ben likes to state it often. Not everyone in Armageddon believes in Sam. Dog and I have observed other people lying about believing in Sam. I have asked Dog previously if dogs believe in Sam, but all he states is, "It's complicated."

In Texas, all these Questions about believing or not believing were called *religion.*

We are close to the riverbank when Dog and I start looking for the location of death for the hero Big Dick McGee. I am not sure where that location is perfectly, so I point to a spot next to a big rock and I state to Dog, "This is called the scene of the crime."

Dog shakes his head. "It's a rock."

Accordion to the famous detective Encyclopedia Brown, someone often would leave pieces of bread on the ground that led to a clue. The crumbs often ended near a person with red hands. I am trying to explain this to Dog but he is sniffing at a large insect perched on the rock. When it flies away, Dog gives chase for a few steps, then barks at it as it flies away. I observe the water is presently the colors of silver and gold because the river is reflecting the light of the morning sun. Again, this is because of science. I do not remember perfectly, but I believe the books in the basement of Carnegie have a story of an old wizard named Roy G. Biv who could control all the colors of the rainbow. (I do not know what the initial G. stood for.)

It is a clear morning. In the distance I can observe Mount Megiddo, where the Dragon lives. What lies beyond the mountains is another Question with no answer. The old maps of Texas display it was called New Mexico, but the whole world changed after the War. Ben has traveled to many places across the Alabama Sea and even to the lands past Old Mexico, but even Ben has never climbed over the rocks of Mount Megiddo and seen what is on the other side. When I am older I will be the first explorer. Dog and I will be the very first to observe what lies on the other side of the mountains. We will come back and be heroes for telling everyone what is there. Sometimes when I dream at night I see green trees and cool breezes and pickup trucks gliding up and down paved streets all day and night. Sometimes I see a girl. When I tell Hyatt about my dreams he states I am dreaming of *paradise*, which is another word for happiness.

Dog states, "Stop daydreaming." He sniffs the ground next to the rock I have pointed out as the scene of the crime. "This just smells like more desert to me."

I state, "We need to observe for clues. We should observe for small pieces of bread, too."

Dog yawns. "This is stupid. I've got goats to chase around." He begins to walk back.

I state, "You can do that later. We must search for the person with red hands."

Dog stops and turns to observe me. "Red with blood?"

I am trying to remember what Encyclopedia Brown would do when he found someone with red hands. "Perhaps. But in Texas, red hands were often a clue."

Dog states, "I think we should go back and ask people in town if they know anything. We should start with Tiny. His hands are often red with blood."

Tiny is in charge of the farm animals of Armageddon. I state, "This idea is not good. Besides, the old people never listen to me."

"Let me take care of that. If you bark at people a few times, they listen."

We find Tiny at his hut, working. Previously he was one of Ben's heroes, but he lost a leg on a previous adventure, when it was eaten by a Demon. Hyatt, who is a wizard, replaced the leg with a metal pipe. Even with one leg, Tiny is the biggest person in Armageddon, therefore I think his name is another lie.

He looks up at me from his table. "You counting heads again, Kid? Well, I'm here, okay? Alive and kicking. Another day in paradise, right?" He goes back to chopping the meat with a huge knife. There is a lot of blood all over the table, and his hands. "Okay, you two have fun out there."

I am about to leave, but Dog pushes his nose into the back of my knee.

I state to Tiny, "Also, we're detecting Big Dick McGee."

"What the Hell does that mean?"

I open my notebook. "Our first Question is, why was Big Dick McGee outside the wall in the night time?"

"Oh, that. Well, I don't know nothing about that. Matter of fact, I don't know nothing about nothing."

There is a long silence before I state, "You are supposed to give us a clue. Like Encyclopedia Brown."

Tiny spits into the bloody dirt by his foot. "And who the fuck is Encyclopedia Brown?"

Dog growls at him. Suddenly Tiny's face turns into a smile. "Oh, you two wanted a *clue*. Why didn't you say so?" The giant man closes one eye, which displays he is thinking more than usual. "I'll give you a clue that's gonna break this case wide open. You ready?" He points to my notebook and leans closer. He covers his mouth with his large hand. "It was Colonel Mustard. In the study. With a lead pipe."

I am writing all this down, but Dog is pulling on my trousers. He states, "Let's go."

The next person we find is Cookie, who is in charge of all the hemp, which means she is in charge of a fuck-ton of things: clothes, rope, food for Dog and the farm animals, and of course medicine. (Cookie is a woman, which is an old girl.) I am sure I will find a clue here because at night,

Hyatt often states he is going to visit Cookie's hut, to repair the plumbing. (In Texas, plumbing meant metal pipes inside the walls for water and feces.) But the only place in Armageddon that contains pipes in the walls is Carnegie, so this is obviously a lie.

I state to Dog, "Cookie is presently our prime suspect."

I knock on her doorway. There is no door. When she comes to the doorway, I note in my book that she is not wearing any clothes to cover her skin, just tattoos. This is normal for Cookie.

"Good morning, Cookie. We're counting alive persons again. Also, we need a clue about Big Dick McGee. And now, someone named Colonel Mustard."

She is smoking weeds, which is unusual because it is morning and in Armageddon medicine is usually taken at night, after the work is done. I write this down as well.

"Well, I'm still alive all right, Kid. In fact, pretty sure it's my birthday today." Her voice sounds like she is coughing. "Now as far as Big Dick, I don't know diddly-squat about that."

I observe my list of words I do not understand and write down *diddly-squat.*

Cookie laughs, the weed-smoke coming out of her mouth in little clouds. She is observing the sky. She states, "I do know this: the name *Big Dick* was a big-ass lie." Big-ass was the French way to refer to something as *extremely* big. This receives my attention. I observe Dog, and he observes me at the perfectly same time so I know it has also received his attention. I rub my chin, because that is what you do when you are detecting. I state, "Cookie, I know Dick is another way to say Richard. Are you stating Big Dick McGee was not his real name?"

Dog nods his head. Finally, a clue.

Cookie smiles. "Sure, Kid. That's exactly what I meant. Got it on good authority his name should've been Pee-Wee." When she laughs again I can see all the holes in her yellow teeth. Her tongue is black, probably from the medicine or perhaps just from being old. She reaches out and puts her fingers into my hair. "But why don't you come inside and relax, Kid. It's my birthday, so I'm taking the day off. You hot? I got cool water out back in the washtub. I could scrub that cute little back of yours, wash your troubles away."

Dog growls.

She takes a step back. "Just a suggestion. Don't be so touchy." She goes back inside the hut. "Sam be with you, and all that happy horse-shit."

We walk back towards Carnegie but I am having difficulty walking rapidly, because something Cookie stated is making me think with one eye open. Dog asks what I am thinking.

I state, "It is Cookie's birthday today."

Dog barks. "So what? It's just a day, like any other day."

But now I am sad. "But don't you wish you had a birthday of your own?"

"I am a dog." He licks at his dirty paw. "Every day is my birthday."

To be honest, I wish I had a day to call my own, like all the old people of Armageddon. They were born before the War, so they possess their own birthdays to celebrate once every year. (A year was three hundred and sixty-five days in a row, because of the sun, which is more science.) In Texas, when you were a boy and it became your birthday, you were allowed to do anything you wanted. People brought you gifts and you ate cake and drank a dark liquid called Coca-Cola. But I do not know my birthday. Perhaps an Alien boy has no birthday.

Ben often states to me that Sam, who is the God, did not know his birthday, either. I wonder how Sam felt when he was my size, growing up in the Holy Land? (Holy Land is another way to say North Dakota.) Did he feel sad, too, when he discovered he did not possess a day of his own?

That is a big-ass religious mystery, for certain.

I am told I was found as a smaller child in the mountains by Ben. I do not know my age. I have no real name. I do not know where I come from, or where I am supposed to be going. But I know I am special. There must be reasons why I am here. Example: when all the old people die, I will still be here to speak with the animals.

But I want a name. I want a story of my own.

Dog and I have detected many mysteries together, but to be completed honesty, I am observing now that the biggest mystery in Armageddon might be: Me.

At dusk, the alive persons of Armageddon are standing in the shallow water of the river to say goodbye to Sassy McSasserton and Big Dick McGee before their spirits travel up to Disneyland. (I am not putting Sassy's name into quotations any longer because I cannot be sure if her name was real or not, and I feel no one should die without having their own name.) Dog and I watch from a distance as they place their wrapped bones onto a raft made of hemp bales, lashed together by Cookie. The old people push it out until the water catches it and sends it slowly down the wide river. The bones are wrapped in hemp leaves, too, which will burn rapidly. Ben wades out downstream and pours gasoline onto the raft as it passes him. (Gasoline is a rare liquid made from the blood of trees and Dragons that is buried deep in the ground. Once we possessed a well inside Armageddon for gasoline, but it dried up.) Suddenly the raft is on fire. Dog and I are standing behind the carts on the shore, watching the flames get higher.

Dog states to me, "Ben is praying." We cannot hear what he is praying but I observe it is a prayer to the God because Ben is holding the palms of his hands together, which is the signal for prayer. Dog and I search the sky, waiting for the bird to appear and take the spirits of Sassy and Big Dick away to Disneyland. I am wondering if they will both leave together, or if they will take turns. But there is nothing moving along the river, not even the little insects or large wading birds that stand in the mud, waiting to shoplift fish. Everything is still.

When this was Texas, there were birds everywhere. You would see birds every day.

Dog points his paw to the horizon and states, "There is a bird." I observe the sky where he is pointing. We are both very excited. Soon I recognize a tiny black dot there, but it is still too far because I do not possess the keen eyes of a dog. The dot gets closer and when it is large enough to display its wings, we stop being excited because we observe it is certainly not a bird, but something lost from the Graveyard. It could be a Lawyer, or perhaps a Telemarketer.

One of the heroes named Lowe, who is always nervous, states, "We got company, Ben."

From the river, Ben observes the flying thing, too, and he lifts his rifle off his back and fires two shots straight up in the air. The black thing turns and heads back towards the Graveyard, where it belongs. Before it disappears, it makes a scream like a rusty wheel turning. Ben states back to the thing, "Not today."

The raft has started to fall apart from the flames and the bones of Sassy and Big Dick disappear under the smoke into the deeper water. Now all the alive persons turn away and come back to shore to begin to unload the long boats. One by one, they slide into the water. They are made of aluminum, which is a metal. I help with Ben's boat. This is hard work, and soon we are all covered in sweat—except for Dog, who does not sweat because he is a dog. Once the boats are all loaded with their gear, I observe the sun starting to dip behind Mount Megiddo. Accordion to Ben, if the sky was red at the end of the day, the sailors of the old world found happiness. This was called a *saying*, which was another way to make magic. I am hoping the sky becomes red tonight, so Ben will be happy. In Texas, he was a sailor at the same time he was a superhero, which is probably why he had more than one name.

Ben stops to wipe his forehead. "Day like this, a man could sure use a cold beer."

"*Beer*," Hyatt states. "Yuck. Pure goat piss." He spits into the river. "You want something cold, try bourbon on ice. That is, if we *had* some ice. Ain't that right, kid?"

I nod, taking out my book and pencil from my pocket, to add *goat piss*.

THINGS HYATT STATES WHEN HE IS ANGRY (OR PRETENDING TO BE ANGRY.)

1. "Aw, horse piss" (Variations: donkey piss, cow piss, sheep piss, and one time, orangutan piss. An orangutan was a primate that once lived on an island named Sumatra. It was not orange.)

2. "Does a bear wear a funny hat?"

3. "You're about as stupid as two mules fucking a washing machine, you know that?" (This is my favorite thing that Hyatt states because it makes no sense.) Fucking means make sex, and a washing machine was a robot that could wash clothes or eating utensils. Ha!

4. "You're about as stupid as two gorillas fucking a tuba, you know that?" (This is my second favorite thing that

Hyatt states because it also makes no sense, and a washing machine seems funnier than a tuba, which was a fat musical instrument.) Sometimes when we are bored, Dog and I try to bother Hyatt in his workshop, just to hear him state loudly about gorillas.

When the boats are loaded fully with everything they will need for a long voyage, all the people sit on rocks and eat hemp seeds and drink water boiled previously. I observe Cookie and Hyatt smoking weeds and talking to one another, and I write this in my book under *clues* for the detection of Big Dick McGee. Silently I try to move closer so I may hear if they are discussing lies about plumbing. After their smoking is completed, Hyatt states loudly to Ben, "You'd better hurry, old buddy. We got about an hour of daylight left out here."

Ben points to the sacks tied down on the boats. "You able to get everything?"

Hyatt states, "Does a bear wear a funny hat? It's all there, amigo. You got everything you need. Gunpowder's all new, and I fixed the action on your shotgun. I even got lucky and finished the Big Nasty I told you about. I'm telling you, this shit makes TNT look like a firecracker. Back in the day, we called it Semtex." He looks up and closes one eye. "I remember one time, in Belfast—"

Ben interrupts Hyatt's history. "I told you, I don't want to know about that stuff. I don't want to know anything about what you did in those days."

Hyatt spits again. "Yeah, I'd better be careful. I don't want to end up in Hell for all my sins." Hyatt's voice contains something called *sarcasm*, which is another word for a lie. I add it to my list. I observe Ben and his men are dressed completely in black. In Texas this was the color of fat people, but Ben is not fat. All the boats are painted black inside and out. I am told this will make it difficult for sea monsters to see them in the dark night. I am proud to state I helped paint the second boat, which is named "Pinta." Ben has told me stories of sea monsters with tentacles the size of large transportations.

He comes over to me and puts his big hand on my shoulder and states, "You stay out of trouble while I'm gone. And stay away from the graveyard."

I nod my head. "We will be busy detecting why Big Dick McGee was outside the wall after dark."

Ben takes a deep breath. Then he states, "Big Dick going over the wall ain't a mystery, Kid. He went over because he wanted to. When Sassy died, well—he kind of died too. Sometimes people just give up."

"I do not understand."

"Sometimes the pain gets to be too much." He turns his head to observe the yellow sky. It is empty but he stares anyway. "Especially when you find yourself trying to survive a God-forsaken place like this. When you get a little older, I think you'll understand."

I state, "When I get older, all the old people will be gone and I will be alone."

Ben smiles. "Sounds like paradise to me, Kid." He turns to his men who are waiting and whistles. "Okay, let's roll." The heroes rapidly push the boats into the water and lift themselves inside. They seem eager to begin the long voyage. Their boats are heavy with gear, and the sides sway up and down as the heroes find their seats and lift out their oars. Ben is holding the tiller of the last boat.

Hyatt states loudly, "If you dipshits find some Jack Daniels floating out there, make sure you bring it back." He laughs so hard he sounds like he is going to be sick so Dog and I laugh too, even though Jack is yet another person we do not know. When Hyatt stops being sick, he turns to me and states, "Pardon my French, Kid."

I feel I should state something loudly, too, so I call to Ben, "Sam be with you."

He waves his hand in the air. "Thanks, Kid. Stay close to Dog. I'll see you again soon."

Dog barks four barks very slowly, almost like growls but sad. This means goodbye.

Ben states loudly back, "Watch out for the Kid, Dog. After all, he's the only one we got."

The boats follow in each other's wake downriver as if they are on a string, the current pulling them towards the Alabama Sea. The water is calm and slow. I observe a little fish jumping near the shore. At this moment the place feels peaceful, and I wonder if it was perfectly the same when this was place was called Texas, before the War. I am imagining a paved road along the edge of the shore, right here, where pickup trucks could drive either way on the river bank or just stop, to allow the boys and girls to make sex on the seat when the sun went down.

Dog stands beside me and states, "You're daydreaming again."

"Yes, I was dreaming of what this riverbank looked like before the War."

He rests his head against my trousers. "Were there many dogs here?"

I nod my head. "They liked to ride around in transportations, too. Sometimes in the back, sometimes in the front with the girls." Suddenly I feel something wet and wiggling inside my trouser leg. It is another fish. Dog laughs his dog laugh, dancing back and forth on his four legs in the shallow water. I begin to laugh too, but I do not splash because I am afraid it may attract something from the deep water. The fish flops down onto my foot, slapping the mud with its tail before it disappears back into its home.

Hyatt states loudly, "All right. Getting dark out here early, people. Let's load up quick and bring it on home."

Dog and I stand with our toes in the cool water, still watching the boats as they disappear around the far bend in the river. The old people left behind are already turning the wagons around, and we must run after them to catch up. I climb onto the back of the last wagon while Dog runs up ahead of the horses, sniffing for trouble in the growing shadows of the desert with his dog nose. In the distance, Mount Megiddo looks like a dark tooth now, the tired sun falling behind it. As we start back to Armageddon, I am still looking behind us, watching the river, even though the boats are now gone. They will be on the Alabama Sea before morning. I observe the surface of the river is smooth again, forgetting the funeral pyre and the wake of the boats already.

I lift my arm and wave my hand back and forth in the air, because in Texas this was how you stated goodbye.

II.
Divide the Waters From the Waters

Through the stinging rain, he could see a horse and rider standing on the grey shore, watching them. The three longboats pitched and yawed with the storm, the thick red algae from the shallow Alabama Sea churning with the waves, staining the whitecaps dark crimson, the color of old blood. Thirteen straight days of calm seas and steady northeast winds, until now; this morning they finally sighted the Appalachians and suddenly there was a wall of black clouds rolling behind them and spitting thunder, as if God had changed his mind at the last moment. Ben wiped the rain from his eyes and muttered to himself as he held onto the tiller: *Wouldn't be the first time, Lord.* From the prow, Smokey whistled back to him and jabbed his sounding pole to starboard: about a hundred feet off, a jagged string of rocks, or maybe rotted wood from an old dock, trying to hide just beneath the surf. Ben nodded and leaned into the tiller with all his weight, the boat slowly responding. The sail was next to useless in this, but it was better than the oars. Even with three men bailing with scoops and buckets, the water in their boat was ankle deep, and rising. "*Watch those rocks*," Ben shouted to the two boats behind him, but the sound of the surf crashing onto the stone beach ahead drowned any voices. Ben turned and gave a hand signal for a hard tack to port instead, and both boats signaled back.

Four days ago, they had already lost one boat to the sea. It happened in the middle of a moonless night, where old maps say Louisiana used to be. In the darkness, floating on a calm sea, Ben had heard the sound of aluminum ripping behind him; seconds later, he heard nothing but the lonely creak of his own boat. No screams, no splashing, no trace: four men and a twenty-six foot whaler swallowed by a shallow sea, with nothing to show for the loss. Maybe it was better to die that way, Ben thought later: after all, four men flailing for their lives in these waters would attract a lot of attention, and then none of the boats would leave that stretch of sea alive. Yes, there were good reasons his entire crew laughed at the idea of life jackets.

Two days later, under a bright waxing moon, they had passed the old statue of Vulcan that still stood over what was once Birmingham. The cast-iron god used to stand on a grassy hill above the south side of the city, but now the Alabama Sea had made Red Mountain a lonely island, surrounding the rusted titan on his pedestal and giving him no escape, eternally calling him back to the sea. At Vulcan's feet, the city was now a flat, shallow grave, with only a few shards of twisted metal and concrete sticking out of the water to remind anyone left that years ago, a million people once lived here. Back when people had reasons to count the years and months. Now there was only day, and night: no need for calendars, or seasons, or expectations. Ben had spent some time on these streets as a college kid down the road in Tuscaloosa, training with the NROTC on the Denny quad, sitting in a classroom in Morgan listening to some old crone drone on about Shakespeare, or eating Chik-Fil-A every afternoon at the Ferg. This part of his memory was sharp: he could even remember the girl who sat across from him one day at lunch, her red hair billowing over her shoulders like a house fire.

There were other things he couldn't remember at all.

In the soft moonlight, he had sat against the gunwale of the boat and looked out at the drowned streets of Birmingham, half-believing the cars and people he saw milling about tonight were real. But he was used to the ghosts. He eased the tiller to port, wondering what day it would be. He went with Tuesday: a weekday it was once called, a workday. He could recall Wednesday was called *humpday*. So many silly names for everything back then: the days, the months, the years. None of which mattered anymore. Ben had gazed out on the shallow graveyard of the city as the boat glided past, keeping his eye out for water hazards ahead. Like so many times since the War, he found his eyesight and memory melting together, his mind still not coming to grips with the insane idea that the world had simply stopped, without warning. He wondered what time it would be on Tuesday: maybe two or three in the morning, a few hours until the red slash of dawn. His crew slept soundly on the deck in front of him. Ben tried to remember the last time he actually glanced at a clock or a phone to check the time. He'd managed to keep his Navy-issue dive watch for a while after the War, maybe a few years even; but there was no need to keep track of time now, in this new world. Time had been erased, just like everything else: the buildings, the roads and the people, all merely plastic things built in a world convinced that everything was permanent.

That night, the three boats had slipped through the ruins unnoticed, following what was once Abraham Wood Boulevard, gliding twenty feet or so above the drowned concrete. Ben found the humor in looking both ways out of habit as the boat passed each intersection. A few crumbled concrete blocks reminded him the Interstate used to run right here, through the heart of the city. They had called Birmingham the *Magic City*, but now it was all gone: thirty years or so ago the War had flattened everything, and then the rising sea went to work in reclaiming it.

In that pale light, Ben had watched Vulcan salute them with his raised arm as the corroded god slowly sank into the dark horizon. Every so often Ben would turn back until all he could see was Vulcan's outstretched arm above the saltwater, a drowning man waving a final goodbye. Ben had silently waved back as they left Birmingham behind and continued east, towards Talladega.

Now, as the three boats bounced their way onto the rocky shore, the storm seemed to subside as quickly as it had come on a few hours ago. The men jumped out to haul the boats from the surf, protecting them from the hungry tide. Ben lashed the tiller on his boat and slid over the side. He kneeled down to touch the solid earth beneath his feet and muttered a short prayer. *Thank you, God. Thank you.* When he rose again, he could see the same horse and rider down the beach, keeping a distance; the stock of a long rifle balanced lazily on the rider's knee. He wore a black oilskin slicker that flowed to his ankles, with a deep hood that covered all of the rider's face except for the hint of a stubbled white chin. Both horse and rider seemed indifferent to the rain. After a moment, the rider silently edged his mount forward as the company began to untie their gear, appearing to ignore him for the moment while they quietly unpacked their weapons from the boats first, preparing for a fight. Ben knew they could have landed on any of the Appalachians; there were hundreds of islands along the chain, and Ben was pretty sure none of them rolled out welcomes for strangers, human or otherwise.

Especially otherwise.

Out of the corner of his eye, Ben took a longer look at the rider's gun: it was an old bolt-action hunting rifle, and it obviously had seen better days; if the thing worked, it probably didn't work very well. Still, he might have another tucked under that loose slicker, Ben thought; and worse, he probably has friends tucked into the rocks above.

Ben smiled. After all, this was an old story for him, the stranger in a strange land.

He held up an open palm to the rider. "*Hello,*" he called out in the friendliest voice he could muster. "Is this Talladega?" he said, pointing down to the rocks at his feet. There was no answer, just the sound of the horse's wet exhale. Ben tried again. "Do you work for the man named Pike?" The rider continued to sit still, the horse only moving to lift a hoof and slap it down on the damp rocks.

Smokey moved closer to Ben and covered his mouth with his hand. "I think we landed on the Isle of Mimes," he said, and a few of the men laughed.

"Yeah, or maybe Monks," Ox said. "They got that vow of silence."

The man named Low joined in. "Monks used to make beer, right? Maybe we're in the right place, after all."

Finally the rider pulled his hood back. His head was clean shaven and there was a deep valley of a scar that ran all the way from his forehead, around his left ear and down to his neck. It was shaped like a crescent moon. He was working a thick wad of something in his mouth; Ben could smell the sweet scent of tobacco, and his empty stomach lurched with the scent.

The rider spoke in a lazy drawl. "Well, you all sure don't talk like no raiders."

Smokey looked around the desolate cliffs above them. "You get a lot of people stopping by, do you?"

The stranger winced, and spat a black comet of chaw on

the ground. "We got worse problems than *people* around here, friend."

Ben stepped forward, both his hands in the air now. "I think that's why we're here, friend. My name's Ben Wolf."

The rider slowly nodded his head. "I've heard of you," he said. "Pike said you'd be coming. My name's Coe—not that it matters much. I'll get someone to take care of your boats." He spat out tobacco again. "That is, if you're still able to come back for them."

"Funny," Ox said. "No wonder they got trouble here. They got a comedian for a coast guard."

Coe let out a wicked laugh, showing his ragged yellow teeth. He gently kicked his heels into the horse and it spun around. "Don't forget to tip your waitress on your way out, friend." He turned back to Ben, pointing into the gloom with the barrel of his rifle. "Ben Wolf, you'll find the Big House up the road a spell, about a mile."

Ben felt someone watching them from the cliffs above. He looked up to see the black outline of someone watching from high atop the cliff, but in a second the shadow vanished. He pointed to the cliffs and called to Coe. "You can call off the welcome reception you got up in the rocks now."

Coe shot him a puzzled look, then he turned to scan the cliffline himself. "If you saw someone, mister, he ain't with me."

"We'll take your word for it," Ben said, turning back to the boat. "Sam be with you."

The words made Coe stiffen; he jerked the reins to draw his horse backwards a step. "We don't believe in that stuff here, mister," he said. "And best not mention any of that Sam stuff to Pike. He goes batshit if anyone mentions Sam or God or North-fucking-Dakota or any of that new age hokey-pokey shit. I'm here to tell you all, he's killed men for less."

"Thanks for the tip," Ben said, turning away.

Smokey handed him his pack from the boat and leaned closer. "I saw that shadow on the ridge, too. Didn't look like no man to me."

Ben nodded, hoisting the pack over his shoulders and tightening the straps. It was heavy from the bulky metal box that held the blocks of Big Nasty that Hyatt had given him, along with the detonators. He slipped his pump-action shotgun from its cover and checked the action, ratcheting a shell into the chamber with a satisfying click. He walked past each man as they all checked their gear over; aside from some leftover seasickness, they all seemed pretty frosty. Ben whistled and they slowly fell in behind him, a company of twelve in a staggered single-file making their way carefully towards the cliffs.

"Good luck to you," Coe shouted after them with a sneer. "You're sure gonna need it."

Ahead, there was a crumbled asphalt path that switch-backed up the steep cliff. "Smokey, take point," Ben said, and his friend jogged up ahead. "Low, you're anchorman again." Low nodded and shortened his step to fall behind the others, looking over his shoulder now and again as they climbed the steep trail.

At the top the old road flattened out into a great meadow. They could see the skeletons of half-dead pine trees ahead.

Ox sniffed the air. "You know what, I'd give my right arm to see a healthy tree for once. Whole world out there, got to have one decent forest still on it. Hell, I'd even take a healthy bush."

"Yeah, we know you'd take a healthy bush," someone else muttered, and they all laughed.

"Cut the chatter," Ben said. "We got a job to do."

Lying along the side of the road in tall milkweed was a battered metal sign, filled with bullet holes. When they got closer they could read WELCOME TO TALLADEGA NATIONAL FOREST. *Hard to believe this was once a state park*, Ben thought; back in the old world, it was a remote piece of Alabama's high country, a few miles off the Interstate and at least three hundred miles from any ocean. Now it was beachfront property, and the Appalachians had gone from mountains to islands. Ben stopped at the fallen sign and kicked it as they passed; he figured he should be used to moments like this by now. But it was always a shock to see reminders of the old world: signposts, house foundations, echoes of cemeteries, husks of cars. Once they found a 1967 Fastback Mustang in a dead oak tree, keys still in it.

He had seen New York City from the water a few years ago, but it didn't much look like New York, or even a city. Another thousand years, or maybe only a hundred the way this world was falling apart, and it probably wouldn't look like anything at all. Every place they went, it was like the world couldn't wait to start over, to clean every last detail away for the next occupants.

"Hey, I think I came up here once to go camping, when I was a little kid," Low called from behind. He stopped a moment to look back over the cliff top at the snarling sea they had left behind. "Always hated camping out back then. Fucking mosquitos would eat you alive. I think we made smores. Can't believe this used to be the fucking mountains, man."

"Still is, I guess," the squat man who went by Shaggy replied. "It's just half underwater now, is all."

"Listen to the professor over here, dropping science," Ox said. "You sound like the Kid."

Low laughed. "Ouch. Just go ahead and call the guy retarded, while you're at it."

Ben turned and walked backwards for a bit. "Last time: let's cut the chatter. And you know damn well the Kid ain't retarded. He's—well, he's *special*."

Ox nodded, but he wouldn't let go, not just yet. "Yeah, special *education* maybe." He put a hand up to his ear. "Hear that, boys? That's the short bus, pulling up."

Ben locked eyes with the bigger man. "I said knock it off." Ox went silent, looking down at the worn road.

As they approached the tall row of pines, Smokey gave a shrill whistle from up ahead. Ben could see something like a wall looming behind the trees. "All right, gents, get frosty."

They all clicked safeties and spread out along the winding road. A few men drifted off the road and picked their way quietly through the tall grass of the meadow. A wind had picked up and now the rain seemed to come at them from all directions. About two hundred feet ahead, Smokey drifted off the path and disappeared silently into the dark pines.

As the rest of the company passed into the cover of trees, the rain and wind died to only echoes. It was midday but inside the dense web of dead branches it was as dark as twilight, the endless tangle blocking out the sky.

Suddenly there came a low growl, coming from the woods to their left. Out of instinct, they all crouched and pointed their weapons into the darkness, scanning left to right for any sign of movement. Nothing

Again, there was an animal snarl. It sounded close, too close.

"You assholes hear that?" Shaggy whispered. "They got bears out here, or what?"

"That ain't no bear," Ben said, the back of his neck shuddering as he peered out into the endless maze of trees. "Listen up. Pike's compound should be just on the other side of these woods," he said, stepping sideways down the path, as if walking a trapeze rope. "Let's move." Slowly they followed him, keeping their guns trained.

Ben could feel the pump of adrenaline making his heart beat faster. For a few hours there, he had actually forgotten why they had come here in the first place. He remembered the message he had gotten from Pike, six months ago. The two men who had brought it to Armageddon over the Alabama Sea had told him the story, but the letter itself consisted of only five words, etched on the back of a piece of tree bark: *MONSTER—COME TO TALLADE-GA—PIKE.*

I hide behind the largest tree trunk and watch the newcomers move along the forest path. I have to bite down on my hand to keep from laughing. They are fools, just like the rest. Their weapons will mean nothing to me. I am getting used to their scent; I have been their shadow ever since they landed on the eastern shore of the island. I always follow from a good distance. Mother says I move so well for someone so big. Once in a while I let out a howl, to let them know they are not alone. They smell like the sea, but also the dry musk of the desert. The desert! If they have come from the east, then that means only one thing: they have come here from the dry plains of Armageddon.

Mother, you will be wondering where I have gone.

Oh, I could smell them before they arrived. A peculiar stench. I watched them from the cliff top as they rammed their longboats onto the beach; my beach. This is my island now, and when I cross the Alabama Sea it will become my sea. I claim it all. This world belongs to me.

Their boats looked sturdy enough. Their coming was no coincidence. This had to be a gift! I want to laugh out loud! But these strangers will hear me for sure. Perhaps I will growl instead, show them what they will get.

I am not the monster. I am not the thing that goes bump in the night. I am much more than human. The world has ended: I am the ruler of what is left. I am the last King. Everything I touch and see are gifts from my Father. Everything I want is a present from God, to help me complete the last leg of my journey—of our journey.

Mother, you will be wondering what I have been doing with myself.

The strangers will soon disappear down the path, on their way towards the compound. I breathed in deeply one last time, taking pleasure in their foreign scent. It was delicious. Tonight I will kill these newcomers, just like I have killed the others. Tomorrow I will take one of their boats and sail west, to find the mountains above a place called Armageddon.

I know I am not meant to die here. I cannot die; I am the last Son of the God. I am the lone sovereign creeping over what is left of the earth, shipwrecked here in Talladega only temporarily. I am the last God, and I will do anything I wish.

Now these new men on the road laugh about something, angering me. I will let out a growl and frighten them. With every one of their voices I hear, the sign on my forehead throbs in pain. My face is still covered with the blood of the two men I murdered in the night.

Mother, you will be so proud of me now.

Tonight, I will return to the sea cave and tell her the good news; now we can leave. She will be happy. She will sing me to sleep with a lullaby. She knows I am not a monster. She knows I have the blood of God running through my veins. She knows I can finally fulfill my destiny.

Pike sat at the far end of a long hall, oozing out of an ornate wooden chair that was far too small for his sagging body. Even from a distance Ben thought the man looked like a fat peacock, dressed in layers of brightly-colored robes that flowed down to his bare feet. His round face was colored, too, with deep black charcoal around his eyes and white streaks like bolts of lightning striking his puffed cheeks. Twisted shocks of white hair sprouted straight out from his skull in every direction, like flares from a dying sun. A pruned peacock, for certain, Ben mused; if his men didn't eat something soon, they might pluck this buzzard right off his throne and roast him on a spit.

The old bird's chair was flanked by two others: a woman with long, white hair sitting with a straight back on his right and a small man with a shaved head, hunched over and on his left.

The half-dozen or so men that stood at the main door to this building were calling it *The Big House*. It stood in the center of the wide compound, surrounded by smaller huts and shanties, an enormous L-shaped patchwork of tall timber and scrap metal. The wall that encircled the compound was simply a fat berm of earth and old logs surrounding everything in a jagged rectangle. This building was massive, but it looked like it could fall down into splinters at any moment. "I don't know what the architect got for this one," Smokey whispered, peering up into the crooked rafters. "But he should have gotten *life*."

None of the others laughed at the old joke; they were too busy craning their necks, taking in all the details of this new place.

The company stood together just inside the doors of the Big House, surrounded by a semi-circle of local men who gawked at these strangers with their fancy guns and gear as if they had come from another planet. Smokey leaned to whisper into Ben's ear. "Is it just me, or does this whole place smell like Death?"

Ben only nodded grimly in response, as he sized up Pike's men that slouched around them. Their weapons looked about as useless as Coe's soggy rifle, down on the east beach. They all looked tired and scared, their eyes half-shut like they all shared the same bad dream at night.

That inhuman growl they'd heard in the forest probably had something to do with that.

The wide compound outside the Big House had reminded Ben of what he'd accomplished back in Armageddon: a loose band of leftover people who carved out a small corner of ground and prayed the walls were tall enough to protect them from all the monsters the War had left behind. There was a sagging watch tower that had been erected above the gate, a twenty-foot wide hole in the wall blocked by an old bus that could be rolled back and forth on its makeshift wooden wheels. The crumpled bus had no windows left but still had the faded *Greyhound* logo with the leaping dog tattooed on its side, sparking a random memory for Ben of a bus stop—there was snow, it must have been the dead of winter, someplace cold—where he once waited for a ride home from basic training, all those years ago. He could almost smell the stale diesel fumes. But it was only a mirage: there was only the thick smoke of cooking fires and the scent of pine needles that comes after a fresh rain.

On the way in, Ben had counted fifty or maybe sixty men and women left here, all with the same haggard and sad, grey faces like some kind of walking dead. And like every other place he had come across, none were under the age of fifty. They were all people born before the War, the same as Armageddon and the half-dozen other outposts he'd come across in his travels. As the company had entered the compound, he had felt all the old eyes turning to stare at them, examining their strange black clothes made of hemp, and their hard faces. It only took a second to realize there would be no warm welcome here, no hospitality for weary travelers. But what use was hospitality in a world that had forgotten about hope?

"Pike will see you now," one of the men at the door announced. He pointed at Ben's chest. "Just you, though. And no weapons, either. You can leave your gear with the others, out here."

"That's not going to happen," Ben replied quickly. "I take what I want. Step aside."

There was a moment when their eyes locked on each other. Smokey was about to put his arm across the guard's midsection to push him away, but the man slowly moved to the side on his own, mumbling something under his fading breath. He looked about the same age as Ben, maybe mid-fifties or so, if this was still a world where people counted the years. But it wasn't. In a way, he looked about a hundred years older. Ben knew anyone still left on this earth was now old, wrinkled and defeated, men and women simply waiting for death. There were no births, there were no children anywhere in this new world. Maybe the craziest detail of this insane world was youth had somehow been erased, just like time and memory. There was only the Kid, and Ben wasn't completely sure if he qualified as human; and even if he was, the boy was definitely different.

Ben turned around to look outside the large doors of the hall, whispering into Smokey's ear. "Looks like they might be hiding something from us," he said, pointing to the odd roundhouse across the compound, pushed up against the wall. On their way inside, Ben had noticed the squat, round building made from stone and mud; it only took a glance to tell it was different from all the claptrap wooden sheds and huts scattered around the yard. This one was much sturdier and had no windows: two sure signs it was either a storehouse or a prison.

"I'm guessing, a prison," Smokey replied, as if he read Ben's mind. There were two stout men with rifles standing in front of the roundhouse door, and another one pacing back and forth along the flat roof.

Ben nodded silently, scratching at his beard. "Let's keep it close for now."

The massive oak doors of the Big House had been carved with what looked to be scenes from old Alabama: two race cars bumping each other in a turn, a football flying through the air of an outdoor stadium, a duck hunter taking aim from behind his blind, all dusty memories of a distant world. But as they had gotten closer, they could see the dark wood was splattered with streaks of dried blood.

Pike's voice echoed through the hall as Ben walked closer. "Ben Wolf, the legend. The dragon slayer, in the flesh. The monster hunter himself, here in Talladega. I can't believe my eyes."

"Oh, you forgot his most important title," the bald man to his left sneered. "Ben Wolf, the infamous back-shooter."

Pike burst into a laugh, his ancient breath wheezing in and out like an accordion. Then he leaned over the side of his chair and slapped the bald man's shoulder. "You got to excuse old Worthy here. We don't get many strangers here."

Ben shot a look back at his men, who were still standing at the doorway, watching him. They were keeping their weapons close, their eyes peering around the dim cavern, alert.

"Yes, forgive our lack of welcome," Worthy said. "But we buried two men this morning."

Ben nodded. "We lost four men to the sea on the way over from Armageddon."

The woman at Pike's right spoke, her eyes sharpening. "A storm?"

Ben turned to her and shook his head solemnly. "No, ma'am. A monster."

"We got a monster, all right." Pike coughed. "I hear you are a religious man, Ben Wolf."

"And I hear you are not."

"You heard right. But monsters have been on this earth way before there was religion, and they'll be here long after."

Ben shrugged, too tired to get into words with someone he'd just met. "But as human beings, we have to look after each other, even now."

Pike laughed. "None of us are human," he said, looking away. "Not anymore."

"I believe there's still a reason we're here."

"You believe what you want to believe," the old man said, jabbing a bony finger at him. "But I don't need no sermon. I need someone to kill a monster. I need a hero. And I do believe you're the last one left."

"Maybe he's not the man for the job," Worthy announced too loudly. He ran his thumb along his chin, peering at Ben with hawk eyes. "All we know is, he's the man who shot our good friend Frank Dayraven in the back."

"Now that is a lie," Ben said. "And everyone knows Frank Dayraven never had a friend in his life." If there was one story that had made its way across this barren earth, it was the day Ben Wolf finally tracked down the killer Frank Dayraven in the Holy Land. It was said that Frank hated

God just as much as Ben Wolf revered Him. That was ten years ago; the tale that had now trickled around the globe, from one mouth to the next, had at least a thousand different versions, each further from the truth of what really happened that sunny day in the Badlands of what was once called North Dakota. It was a nightmare that still woke Ben in a cold sweat, now and again.

Pike leaned forward from his chair, scratching at a snowdrift of hair on the back of his head. "So you didn't shoot him?"

"Oh, I shot him, all right," Ben said, not flinching, even smiling a little. "But not in the back." He looked at Worthy. "Even a fool knows you can't shoot a snake in the back."

At this, Pike roared in laughter, slapping his hand down on his knee. "Ain't that the truth! Old Frank was a snake, all right. Filthy sonofabitch, to boot." He lifted his hand and stretched it out to his right, until it rested firmly on the woman's wrist. "Oh, I like this one, Wilma," the old man said. "He's got guts."

Wilma waited a moment before slapping the peacock's withered hand away. "I can see that," she said. "I want to know if he's got enough guts to kill the monster out there."

Pike hummed a tune under his breath. "That's my wife, working the bottom line. Do you know she was a lawyer, back in the old world? No lie." He stood up on his wobbly legs and pushed himself away from his chair. "Pike says, if you do this thing, anything I have is yours."

Wilma lowered her head into both hands.

"Well, we're not guns-for-hire," Ben said. "We do it for other reasons." He looked back at his company. "But you do have some things around here we don't have back home. Maybe we can make a trade or two before we leave."

Worthy piped up, throwing his slender arms in the air like an actor in a play. "So, you'll kill this monster for nothing? *Please*. Forgive our distrust. You don't even know what we got out there."

"I got a pretty good idea, friend," Ben said. "I saw pretty much everything, in the War."

Wilma interrupted. "You were there?"

Ben nodded. He was growing impatient; his stomach began to grumble. He scratched at the back of his neck. "Maybe you can tell me more about this monster after we eat," he said, waving his arm back at the doorway. "We haven't eaten today."

The whole time he stood there in front of him, Ben could feel the woman Wilma's hot stare pressed onto him. She was weighing him with her sharp eyes, as if he was on a scale and she was charged with guessing his worth. When he finally lifted his eyes to meet hers, they both nodded slightly at each other, as if the two complete strangers knew they shared a dark secret.

I wait for my only friend, the darkness, to come before I slip out the sea cave and into the cool air. Mother is in a fitful sleep now, her tired face still covered with worry. At twilight, I like to watch the edge of the sun dip below the

Alabama Sea, drowning the orange sky in black with the coming night. It is beautiful. It reminds me of happier days. My memory is blurred.

I climb to the top of the hidden cliff path and start east across the dark meadow. Every time it is the same: the closer I get, the more my mind can think of nothing but the kill. They all think I am merely a monster, but Mother knows my secret. I am a god of vengeance and anger, and everyone left on this diseased earth belongs to me.

I have killed more men than I can count now. I am doing my Father's work, getting rid of the last few pieces of leftover trash. I have left my own trail of death from drowned Florence to what was once New York, and now down to these silly islands of the Alabama Sea that had once been mountains. And they dare call me *monster*. Soon everyone will know the truth: I am the only son of the Messiah. I am the Chosen One, a Holy Bastard, the Stepson of Vengeance.

I slip through the tall grass quickly. Ahead, I scare a few cowering birds into the air. In only minutes I reach the canopy of thick trees, just as the stars come out above.

I say, fuck the stars. I am the stars, and the moon, and the sea. I am the Universe, and you all belong to me. Do you hear?

Tonight I will kill these newcomers. After they are gone, there will only be the shallow sea between me and the place called Armageddon. My rumor of Paradise. My destiny of an entire world, beginning again.

I wear the mark on my forehead, the scar of royalty. I claim my birthright. I claim this new world. In the name of God my Father, I claim it all.

Frank Dayraven still haunted his dreams. Ben lay flat on the plank wood floor, his head propped on the box of explosives that Hyatt had sent with him. He was tired, drifting in and out of sleep, but he knew he had to stay alert. Frank Dayraven. That was so many summers, too many to remember how long ago—but the night Ben had finally caught up with him was as vivid in his mind as ever. Frank was known for burning people alive, just for being in his path. The trail of charred bodies and horror stories had led Ben deep into the Holy Land, somewhere outside where Bismarck had once stood. The stars had begun to come out when Ben turned a corner into a twisted arroyo, and there he was, suddenly face to face with the killer. In the recycled dream, Frank's face was always ashen and scarred, already dead. Already food for the buzzards, and probably worse.

Frank had not gotten up from the rock where he was sitting, as if he'd been waiting for Ben to come. *I suppose you come all the way out here for revenge*, he had said in a slow voice.

There's no revenge, Ben remembered saying back. There had been a lump rising in his throat. He remembered trying to edge closer in the dim light. *I'm just trying to do what's right.*

Frank let out a sour laugh, and it had sounded like a caged bird. *There is no more right,* Frank always repeated in the dream. *There is no right, not anymore.* The gaunt man spoke as if they were two old friends finally reuniting; he rubbed at his beard with both hands. *You think you're fightin' for something. But look around. There's nothing left to fight for. Not in this world.*

Ben stood still. *Faith,* he replied. *Faith is worth fighting for.*

In the dream, Frank always looked up as if he'd heard a gunshot. *Faith?* He stood up now, his arms moving about nervously. *Do you even know what planet you're on?*

Ben always woke at this point in the dream, right before he remembered reaching for his gun. The rest of the story only lasted a few seconds anyway. Frank Dayraven had been a cold-blooded killer with no soul, but even so, those words had surprised Ben at the time, and they still echoed in his mind. The image of this man going down coughing blood had not stayed with him; instead, it was the words he spoke that haunted him, the idea that his own life was worth nothing.

As he lay on the hard floor of the Big House, Ben turned his head to look at his men sleeping around him. They were all exhausted from the long journey, and most were snoring loudly.

His thoughts turned quickly to that odd brick and stone building outside the doors. What were these people hiding? What could they have that was of any value?

There could be only one answer. There was only one thing that had value anymore in this world; only one treasure to keep out of sight from strangers, the same way Ben always kept the Kid out of sight when the Travelers arrived in Armageddon, now and again.

The only thing worth anything was *youth*.

Above the snoring, he thought he could make out a low grumbling, an animal growl, from the other side of the wall to his left. Something was prowling out there. He sat up when he heard something scratch the wood. Something wanted to get in. Ben reached behind him for Hyatt's box and opened it slowly.

If there was a monster out there, he would be more than ready.

And if there was indeed a child being held in that round house—another alien child like the Kid—he would have it.

Daylene opened her eyes to a thin shaft of moonlight that filtered into the cave's mouth. She had slept fitfully through most of the night soundly on the hard rock floor, a rare thing. Her son had not returned the night before, and she was worried. She rubbed her eyes and sat up, trying to listen: somewhere in the darkness she could hear him crying, her only son. It was a sound she had never heard, even when he was a small child. She ripped the stolen blankets off her body and felt her way along the rough wall to the mouth of the cave, the sea crashing against the dark beach below.

Then she saw him, crawling towards her in the moon-light.

Her son, sliding slowly in the dirt towards her on the slim path, one arm grasping at the ground, dragging his twisted body forward in agony. The other arm was gone. She went to him, almost falling to the rocks far below in her haste to reach him. She quickly regained her balance and tried to help him to his feet. His massive body dwarfed her. Together they limped back into the dim cave, the embers of a fire shedding just enough light to make out his makeshift bed. He slumped down on his back there, his arm socket still leeching blood, his eyes wide with fear. She gathered all the blankets they had and covered him to his neck. The right side of his face had been burned away, exposing the bone under the charred flesh.

"Mother," he whispered to her, blood clotting his throat. "You told me I was a god."

"You are," she said, sitting and stroking his matted hair. "You are. You're my son."

She sprang up to stoke the fire and find the water bucket, to wash his wounds. It was all she could think of to do. When she returned, her son was dead, his mouth open in a silent scream. She threw her small arms around him and began to cry.

After a moment, her sadness slipped into anger. She was alone, once again. Whatever he was, he had been her only son. Someone had killed him. Someone had taken away the only thing she still lived for in this wretched echo of a world.

Her life didn't matter anymore. There was nothing left, no more promises to keep. Someone—anyone—was going to pay.

Pike's face looked bored as Ben retold the story of the night before. Only Worthy was on the edge of his seat, listening closely. "Where in the world did you get plastic explosives?" Worthy said, his face smiling in disbelief.

"Well, in Armageddon we're lucky to have our own wizard," Ben replied, thinking Hyatt would love to hear that. "And he's got a lot of free time. He also has got a long record of blowing shit up. So we get along just fine."

Wilma and Worthy both laughed as they listened, but Pike just shook his head. "That don't impress me," he said, spitting on the floor in front of him. "Don't impress me at all. I suppose you and your boys will be wanting to leave Talladega." He leaned back, letting out a manufactured yawn. "As soon as you are able."

"We just might," Ben said, smiling himself. "But first, I'd like to ask what you're hiding in that round house back there."

Suddenly, Pike shot up ramrod straight on his brokedown throne. "I—I don't know what you're talking about," he blurted out. "Nothing in there but—well, there's nothing in there. Besides, that's my business." He shifted from left to right. "Hear me? No business of yours."

Ben stood his ground in front of the three. He'd told his men to wait again by the door, but they were all listening. "Two days ago, you said we could do a little trading," Ben said calmly. "If I killed your monster. Well, it looks like I killed your monster. His arm's still lying over there, from last night if you want to take another look."

Pike coughed. "And just how do we know the monster's dead?"

Worthy leaned over and gripped the old man's forearm. "Listen to reason, Pike. There's a trail of blood like a river leading back over the wall," he said. "Whatever that thing was, it's dead now. I'll be the first to say I was skeptical. Maybe even a little jealous. But now, I say we owe Ben Wolf here a debt."

"I agree," Wilma said. She was still sizing up the man standing in front of her.

"Well I *don't*, and I make the rules around here, in case you two forgot," Pike sneered.

Ben let out a grunt, impatient. He wished he was home already, back in Armageddon. "I'll give you until nightfall to decide," he said, turning to the doors. He walked out into the twilight air, glancing at the round house before heading for the gate.

Smokey called after him from the steps of the Big House. "You want company, boss? Getting pretty dark out."

Ben shook his head without stopping. "Tell everyone to stay frosty," he said. "I'll be back in a few. I just need some time alone." He motioned to the tower above the gate, and waited for a few minutes as the Greyhound groaned backwards, opening the gate. He slipped through into the woods outside, taking a deep breath as he wandered off the path into the trees. After a quarter mile or so he stopped, leaning against one of the ruined trunks. He was alone; the forest stood silent in every direction. He looked around before kneeling on the soft ground to pray, closing his eyes. His knees groaned, another reminder that he was an old man, and becoming older with every sunrise. The prayer wouldn't take long, since he only knew one.

O God...

As he whispered the words to himself, he heard a twig snap in the distance. Someone was watching him. He continued as if he had heard nothing, but dropped his hands slowly to his sides.

O Sam...

He could hear nothing now; maybe it was only his imagination. As he lost himself in the words he'd been taught as a young man, he mumbled over and over under his breath, Ben felt the soft weight of a hand pressing his shoulder. Out of instinct, he sprang up as best his creaking legs could, reaching for his weapon before realizing it was Wilma, standing close to him. The moon shone through the cracks of the mottled tree branches above them, illuminating her pale face with jagged slivers of white light. "I followed you out here," she said in a whisper.

"I can see that," he said. "You scared the shit out of me."

"I doubt that," she said. She came closer, putting her hand on his chest. "You don't seem to be the type."

He was startled, but he didn't move away. "What kind of type do you see me as, then?"

She kept her hand on his heart. "I think you're the type with a secret to tell."

"Aren't we all," he said, pulling her hand off his chest.

"I think you know our secret already," she said. "The round house."

They locked eyes, and Ben drew in a deep breath; there was no reason to keep the secret from her, with Armageddon so far away. "We have a boy in Armageddon. As far as I know, he's the only child on earth. But I'm not even sure he is a boy."

"And tell me, this boy," she said, "Is he, different? I mean—well—is he missing some parts?"

Ben stepped backwards, startled. "How did you know that?"

She smiled, deepening the lines in her face. "The round house," she said slowly. "It's a prison, all right," she said. "For a little girl. A little girl that sounds a lot like your boy. She was found on the beach, only a few days ago. Pike has been hiding her in there since you arrived. He has," she said, wincing for a moment. "Other plans for the child."

Ben turned to look into her eyes, trying to process what she'd just told him. "Why are you telling me this?"

"Pike is a fool," she said, kissing him. "I am guessing you are not. Now, I don't believe in your new God—and I'll be the last person left on this earth to try and figure out what we're all still doing here." She pointed behind her, back towards the compound. "But I'm also smart enough to think this can't be a coincidence. Am I right?"

Before Ben could answer, suddenly there were shouts echoing from the compound, shattering the dark silence around them; it was a woman's cry, her long wail in grief. Then, more shouts. Wilma was the first to break into a run, leaving Ben to follow and catch up to her. They both picked their way through the moonlit woods and back on the road to the main gate. Wilma shouted up to the watch tower to let them in, the spooked watchman standing guard taking his sweet time to make sure it was actually her. Wilma banged her palms on the bus before it slowly began to roll back. Without waiting, they both slipped through the open crack and ran towards the steps of the Big House, where a crowd had gathered.

Ben made a path through the gawking masses and saw two bodies lying on the steps, their throats cut. They were both clean slashes done by some kind of knife, that much was clear.

Ben looked at the two faces; he had to close his eyes and turned away. One of them had been his man, Lowe.

Ben opened his eyes again and kneeled to the ground, looking at the dirt. In the dim torchlight, he could see the wet reflection of a thin trail of blood; it led away, directly towards the compound wall. Wilma pushed her way through the crowd to him, her grey eyes suddenly filled with fear. "Are you sure you killed that fucking thing?"

"I don't know," Ben said.

"You don't know," Pike's voice cackled from the doors of the Big House above them. Even with these two corpses in plain view, he sounded like he was enjoying himself. "You see? This is the monster killer we sent for. So much for the *hero*. Guess the world's run out of those, too."

Ben ignored him, his mind filled with questions. Someone would have to follow that blood trail over the wall and find out, he thought. After they found a place to bury old Lowe.

D aylene crept back into the cave with the first crack of morning light, her arms lacquered in dried blood up to her elbows. She was still breathing hard, not from the journey but from the excitement. The knife still felt light in her hand. Finally, she collapsed against the rough wall of the cave, shaking a little with the sweat cooling on her hot skin.

She had *enjoyed* it. She had enjoyed watching those men die.

She had wanted to feel the power of retribution for so long now, the sweet sting that only comes with revenge. She had wanted someone—anyone—else to feel all the pain she had felt her entire life, the weight of loss and longing, and of regret. She felt empty, she realized that now, but for some reason the emptiness felt *good*; maybe it was the only way to feel in this, an empty world.

If this world was Purgatory, she hated to think what Hell was going to look like.

She had stopped counting long ago, but it must have been thirty years since she had seen Sam that day in France, and almost all of that time she'd spent on the run, trying to survive this crazy new world, trying to keep their son alive.

She looked at the blood, caked on her fingers. The only word to describe how she felt at that moment was *drunk*. "Do you see what you've done to me?" she screamed into the darkness, a sliver of her still hoping he would finally answer. "Do you see what I've become?" But there was no answer, only the sound of the waves crashing on the rocky beach below. *I am going back tonight*, she laughed to herself. *I am going to kill until I get an answer.*

She could still recall his voice, hear it echo in her ear. *Thou shalt not, Daylene, and all that shit*, she mumbled to herself, laughing again. She hadn't heard her own name out loud for as long as she could remember. She said it again: *Daylene. Daylene. Daylene*. It sounded so ancient and strange, like a foreign language lifted from some forgotten wall or scroll. She hadn't been that girl for a long time. She dropped the knife to the cold stone floor, and it made an empty sound. She wasn't even a mother anymore, the only part of her that had still felt alive. Now she was a slayer, a revenge-taker. She was the mother of retribution, the abandoned Queen of Purgatory.

Why did you abandon me, so long ago?

She was the monster, drenched in blood.

The trail of blood had led him back to the sea cliffs. Ben had decided to follow it alone. It led him east through the meadow and towards the afternoon sun: drops of blood on open stretches of ground, tiny smears against withered leaves and stems as the killer had brushed by. There were high clouds dotting the yellow sky ahead. He could smell the salt water and see the bright shimmer of the crimson sea ahead.

Pike's words from last night still rang loudly in his head: *So much for the hero.*

He knew he had to finish this alone.

At the cliff face, he noticed a slim footpath, hidden from below, which slanted down across the steep rock wall. From the precipice he scanned the shoreline for the watchman Coe, but there was no one around, in any direction. He descended the razor-thin path, balancing with his hand against the rocks, his feet one in front of the other like a tightrope. After four switchbacks, he could see the trail ending in the dark mouth of a cave. He lifted his sidearm silently out of its holster, pushing the safety off with his thumb. There were a few more specks of blood scattered among the rocks at his feet; this had to be end of the trail.

At the rim of the dark hole, he peered inside, wondering how deep it ran into the cliff. He took a deep breath before taking his first step out of the sunlight and into the black ahead. Before he could take his second, a voice from inside the cave stopped him cold.

"Tell me something, mister. You ever been to North Dakota?" It was a woman's voice.

Ben felt for the ground ahead and took another step, his eyes trying desperately to adjust to the darkness. "I've been to the Holy Land, yes."

There was a sinister laugh. "*Holy Land*," the voice said. "Shit."

"Funny thing was, I always used to think it was a *wasteland*," she said. "But I guess I had no idea what a wasteland was."

Ben slid his back along the cavern wall slowly. "A lot of things changed after the War."

"You're here to kill me," the voice said calmly, without any hint of fear. "You've come here for revenge."

"Two men are dead," Ben said. "One of them was my friend."

"Sounds like revenge to me." The voice sounded closer now, but Ben's eyes still were washed in black. "I guess I'm ready. I just want you to do one thing. Can you do that? Just remember my name. It used to be Daylene Hooker. Can you remember that?"

"Your name," he said, "is *Daylene Hooker*?" Ben froze; anyone who believed in Sam Davidson knew the name Daylene Hooker. He figured she had died and risen to Heaven with everyone else, a long time ago.

"Damn right," the voice said to him. "Don't you forget it." With that, Ben felt a sudden rush of air and before he could react, a figure swept past him and towards the waiting light of the cave mouth. It was a woman, all right, with mottled curls of white hair falling down her back. She was running at full speed towards the cliff face. Ben reached out to grab her, but he was too late. The figure leapt off the lip of the cave and disappeared over the edge, leaving only yellow sky.

At the entrance to the cave, Ben peered down into the jagged rocks, but there was no sign of a body, just the sound of the tide lapping at the rocks. The sea had already taken her back.

At first light, the company had already finished loading their whale boats, anxious for the long journey home. They had waited seven days until the moon had started to wax before starting out, to see better in the night. Ben stood apart from them and watched his men stand in a loose circle and talk excitedly of their adventure, with the voices of much younger men. They were giddy from smoking the last of their weed they'd carried from Armageddon. They had traded a few blocks of Cookie's best product for some bales of Talladega cotton, stacks of pine boards and a dozen ceramic jugs filled with the local corn wine. And one girl.

The Talladega corn wine sure wasn't Jack Daniels, but it packed a punch and they all knew Hyatt would be happy for a swallow. They had buried one jug with Lowe in the high meadow above, hoping their old friend would be able to quench his thirst on his way to Disneyland. *I'm going to Disneyland*, they all chanted over his grave. *I'm going to Disneyland*. It was one of the rare moments when everyone seemed to believe in an afterlife, in a faraway place that waited for them. Might as well be named Disneyland, they thought.

As the men talked and laughed on the beach, Coe sat his horse from a distance, pretty much the same position they had met him a dozen or so days ago. He sat with the old rifle on his thigh, chewing another thick plug of tobacco and spitting juice at the rocks below. Ben approached the grizzled coast guard and held out about an ounce of Cookie's gold, wrapped in cotton cloth. "I'll trade you this for a fresh plug, if you have one."

"*Shit*," Coe said, balancing the gun across his saddle to hold the weed up to his nose. "I haven't seen this in a long time. My old girlfriend Mary Jane. Good shit?"

Ben nodded. "The best that Texas can offer the boys of Alabama."

They made the trade. Ben turned away and headed back to join his crew, already cutting off a thick wad of chew with his knife and slipping under his lip. The taste instantly reminded him of his Navy days and the first time he tried to chew tobacco: a green lieutenant at BUDS trying to befriend some enlisted guys by sharing their chaw, and then going lime green in the face after only a few minutes, puking in a fire bucket afterwards. He turned back to the rider one last time, glancing at the sorry rifle in his hand.

"You weren't too sure we'd make it back," Ben called to him, coming back.

Coe smiled his crooked smile. "Let's just say I wasn't lay-

ing no odds on it. But I'm happy you did. Don't know what
I'd do with all these boats messing up my beach, anyway."

"Here," Ben said, unhooking his gun belt and handing it
to Coe. His old Ruger LCP and the twenty rounds on the
belt would be an upgrade from that dirty musket he lugged
around. "For the raiders."

Coe let out a shrill whistle, holding the belt in the air
like a prize. "Would you look at that. Roll Tide, friend."

Ben smiled; he hadn't heard that since before the War.
"Roll Tide." It was yet another dusty memory mingled with
his vision, a constant mix of the living and the dead. It felt
good to say the phrase out loud, as if he was still part of
something in this lonely world. He said one last good-bye to
his new friend, then turned to face the wide Alabama Sea.

The girl was standing alone on the grey beach. The
resemblance to the Kid was uncanny: same height, same
piercing eyes, same wiry mess of hair. They could be twins.
As soon as he had seen her emerge from the prison of the
round house, seven days ago, he knew right away this trip
had been no coincidence. There was a reason he had come
here, he was certain of it. He watched as the girl dug her
bare toes into the coarse sand, the gentle surf lapping at her
small feet. She was wearing rough cotton pants and a too-
big shirt, with an old nylon backpack in neon pink hanging
off one shoulder. From Ben's view, she was peering back
and forth along the stretch of shoreline as if waiting for the
school bus to arrive, just as his own daughter did, so many
years ago.

Ben kept watching her as she stepped tentatively up to one of their aluminum long boats, running her small hand along the transom where Smokey was working. She said to him, "We're going to Armageddon in this?"

"Yeah, the private jet is in the shop," Smokey said, helping her into the boat with his good arm. "Can you swim?" The girl gave him a quizzical look, as if this was an exam she hadn't studied for. He motioned with the one arm, demonstrating a kind of side stroke. "You know, swimming?"

"I do *not* know. What is swimming?"

Smokey stared at the strange girl, waiting for the punch line. When there was none, he shrugged his shoulders and went back to his work. "Well, come to think of it, swimming ain't much of a help out there, anyway."

Overhearing them, Ben smiled and turned to take a last look back at the jagged cliffs above, shielding his eyes from the new sun that had just cracked the sky behind them. Wilma was standing there, alone; it was only a dark silhouette but he knew it was her, right on the edge. She waved down to him, and he waved back. In a different world—a previous world, a civilized world—he would have asked her to come with him, and she would say yes. But on this brutal planet, right now all that mattered to him was the girl, keeping her safe and getting back to Armageddon. He realized he didn't know what was happening or why, but he had a feeling he was part of it. There *was* a puzzle, he was certain of it, even if he couldn't tell what the pieces were.

After another moment, he turned back to the company. "All right, gents—and lady—let's shove out. Let's go home." Restless, the men dropped the dying embers of their smokes. They all ·dropped their shoulders and muscled the whale boats into the surf, taking to the oars until they reached the breakwater about a hundred yards out, when they would be able to raise sail. The girl tried to keep her balance in her boat, giggling a little as she enjoyed the jerky ride. With luck, they would take a course of south by southwest and reach Vulcan in two or three days, and then due west in a slow tack over what was once Mississippi, then southern Louisiana, and finally Texas. From the tiller of the *Nina*, Ben checked the compass around his neck for a bearing, looking up to watch the girl lean over the gunwale of the boat and dip her hand curiously into the cool, crimson-stained water. This was all new to her, it seemed: the boat, the sea, the people. She cupped her hand and lifted it slowly, examining the salt water in her hand as if it was for the first time. She held her closed hand up to her nose, sniffing the water before letting it fall back into the sea. Looking at her, Ben decided she could have been the Kid's twin: she had the same dark hair, the same curious brown eyes. And it appeared she was talking to the small fish that danced in the shallow water, so they had talking-to-animals in common, too.

"Can I ask you something?" Ben called to the girl. He still couldn't get over how similar she looked to the Kid, back in Armageddon a thousand miles away. "Do you like to read books, by any chance?"

She looked puzzled. "I don't know," she shouted back. "What is a book?"

This is going to be interesting, he muttered under his breath. "Do you have a name?"

The girl looked lost in her thoughts. "No, I don't think so. Not yet." She went back to staring at the school of swirling fish alongside the boat, talking to them as if they were all old friends. After a pause, she asked blankly, "Do I need a name?"

Ben smiled. "Not really sure."

Satisfied, she went back to talking with the little fish over the side of the gunwale. Ben Wolf leaned on the tiller and wondered what the child was thinking, at that moment. He wondered if she had an idea of what lay ahead, for all of them. It felt like the start of something, the first two pieces of a puzzle that finally fell in line. He wondered if the girl held any clues as to what came next. He only knew that he did not.

LEFT
PAW

RIGHT
PAW

OFFICIAL SIGNATURE
of **DOG**
(recorded by Kid)

III.
The Herb That Yields Seed

This is what I want out of life: to feel the tender pull of flesh in my teeth and taste the hot drip of blood on my tongue. I want to chase something deep into the mountains and corner it, closing in slowly while it whimpers and begs for mercy. I want *pleading*. I want to take down something big: a whitetail deer or a wild boar, and then maybe work up to a yak, if there's any yak left wandering this world. I know I'm not supposed to eye the other animals inside Armageddon like I do. I'm supposed to do the opposite: it's my job to protect the dimwitted chickens and the nervous goats and now, the alien Kid. But sometimes I just feel the urge to bare my fangs and scare the living shit out of something so I can chase it through the wilderness. Is this too much to ask? Why else would the God give me fangs, if not to hunt in the moonlight? Listen: I am no pet. I am a *beast*. I'm the son of wolves and first cousin to hyenas, and what I'm supposed to do when I see you coming is lick my fucking chops.

I am a dog, and this is my right.

In Texas, dogs were once the toughest of all animals. It's all written down in the bottom of Carnegie; a lot of these books the Kid reads out loud are really boring, but if the story's got a dog in it, I'll listen. Old Yeller, now there was a salty dog. In Texas, if you were a tough human, you were called a *salty dog*—sorry, but there was no such thing as a salty lion or polar bear. The toughest soldiers were called dog soldiers. The hardest workers in Texas worked like a dog and the hottest days were called dog days. And guess what guarded the gates of Disneyland, where all the humans go to die? A killer whale? A dragon? Ha! *Amateurs*. A dog with three heads, that's what. But then something horrible happened to the historical dogs of Texas. At the end of the world, they had to be carried in purses and shopping bags. They had *owners*. They stopped running in packs, and the only place dogs were allowed to smell each other was some torture chamber called a *dog park*. Dogs were forced to wear thick sweaters and colorful hats to keep out the cold; what happened to their own fur? Was there a dog-plague at the end of the world that made us all weak and helpless? Dogs were reduced to pets that ate some slop called *dog chow,* spooned out by their owners from cans into a bowl. No wonder dogs got sick.

Listen to me: you do not spoon a dog anything. We are dogs, and we do not eat out of bowls. We are predators, and we take what we want.

I have actually eaten this dog chow from a can. It was called *Alpo*, and it was absolutely poisonous. I couldn't finish it. The human Hyatt traded some travelers a bag of weeds for it and stood there watching me, like this was some kind of reward. It tasted like wet socks. I wish I spoke English so I could tell *him* to eat it.

Yeah, I've tasted wet socks before. I'm a dog.

If I'm the first dog in this new world like Kid is the first kid, I want to be the saltiest dog I can be. I want to be the dog that future generations of dogs look back at and say, *now that was a dog*. A dog that makes even the timber wolves jealous. There will be no owners, and no pets here. There will be no damn dog parks, no leashes. And if anyone tries to put a fucking sweater or a hat on me, I'm warning you right now, this dog *will* go straight for the jugular.

I realize there's got to be some kind of compromise. After all, a working dog just can't run around Armageddon howling with hunger all the time, or ripping into a wounded sheep whenever the flock leaves it behind. That sounds more like a *coyote*, not a dog. Dogs have rules. Sure I'm a beast, but I also pride myself on being a loyal friend and a hard worker. And I can also be silly, when the situation calls for it. Dogs can be silly! You see, a dog has many layers. A coyote only has one layer, the one that says *I need to shove something in my mouth*. Coyotes have absolutely no sense of humor. If you've ever heard a coyote try and tell a joke, then you know exactly what I'm talking about. Yuck.

This much I understand: the old humans of Armageddon need me to protect the Kid. So each day in Armageddon, I choke down the boring food made of plants they give to all the animals, and I drink my water from a bowl, like some cat or hamster. Once in a while I get something extra, like raw eggs or a fish from the river or fresh berries from a bush, and when that happens I do exactly what they expect me to do: I find the nearest human hand and I lick it. Maybe I throw in a sloppy pant or two, with my tongue out, to let them know I'm a happy dog.

There is no humping of a human leg involved. I don't know where that one came from. It's ridiculous, and besides, I have no idea where that leg has been.

Like I said, dogs have rules.

But that doesn't mean I don't want to go a little crazy, now and then.

It's another boring morning and I'm helping Kid detect the mystery of the clue of something or other—oh, right, the murdered chicken in the farmyard. It's all the same to me. Each morning I meet him outside the big stone building they call Carnegie and we try to fill the daylight with things to do. This is what humans call a *routine*. But I'm a dog, and I call it fucking boring. Dogs don't need routines, we need to roam. We need adventure. We need to piss wherever we want, yeah, even if it's on your foot. What I should be doing is help this hairless boy to learn the skills he'll need, like how to pick up a scent left in the mud of the river, or how to clamp his teeth on the jugular of his prey. But instead, all we do is play games and read books. Well, he reads the books and I look at the pictures. I have to listen to this Kid talk big talk about swimming across the river without being eaten, or climbing that mountain to take on a dragon, but when we stand on the riverbank he looks at the water and I know he's afraid. How's he going to survive in this world if he can't hunt down his dinner? How's he going to kill this dragon if he cannot even enjoy killing a water lizard, or a little fish, or a stupid goat?

Dogs grow faster than humans, I guess.

Today we're standing outside the gate to the chicken coop. Kid is writing clues in his paper book as I sniff at the blood stains in the dirt, pushing my nose into the shredded feathers that blow back and forth in the breeze. I can feel the chickens inside the coop all looking at me.

The Kid is looking around. "First question: how did the chicken get outside the gate?"

"I don't know," I say. I want to lap up some chicken blood, but I resist.

He crouches down on his hind legs to get a closer look. "It was not shoplifted, because the bones of the chicken are still here. It was eaten right here in this spot. Who would eat a chicken like this?"

I twist my paw in the dirt. "I don't know." Behind me, I feel a hundred chicken eyes burning into my hair.

But I *do* know. It was me. Last night, I opened the gate and lured that fat chicken right out into the farmyard. It was pure instinct, and I couldn't help it. I wanted to know how it felt to *attack*, to kill my prey. The whole thing was a mess. It was dark and I was mostly going by my ears. I do remember feathers everywhere. There was a chase, but it wasn't much of a chase because as it turns out, chickens run in circles, so all I had to do was stop and wait for this bird to come back around again. And then there was the squawking. Oh, the fucking *squawking*. I remember trying to find its jugular, but then I realized chickens don't have a jugular, so I panicked and my teeth clamped down on its beak instead.

If you've never thrashed a frightened chicken around by its beak, I don't recommend it.

I want to tell Kid that I am the mystery, it was me, but I don't. I know he's not a dog, but he's still in my pack. I don't want to disappoint him. So I keep my big trap shut, which is what I should've done in the first place.

Sure I feel bad for this poor bird, now. But when you are a dog and find your teeth clamped down on a throat, well, the only thing you want to feel is *blood*. Later, after your belly is full, that's when the guilt drifts in. Last night, after it was over, I kept telling myself no one will miss this chicken. But as it turns out, anything can be missed, even a dumb bird that eats bugs out of the ground.

A few minutes later, the Kid is finished with his clues and we're about to leave when the mule named Gus calls me over to where he is standing, by the stable fence. I'm surprised, because the old bastard has never said two words to me since I've been here. The humans call him gloomy. I call him an asshole.

The mule leans his neck over the rail and drops his head down so he can whisper in my ear. "I saw what happened last night, Dog." He jerks his head to flick some flies away from his mane. "To the chicken."

My reaction is very un-dog-like: I act stupid, like a chicken or a goat. "You did? Nice work, mule. I will tell the Kid, who is busy detecting right now. So, who did it, then? Who killed the chicken?"

"Oh, I think you know who did it," he whispers through his big mule teeth. "Should I tell the Kid who did it, too?"

I'm trying to look up into his brown eyes to see what he really knows, but a mule's eyes are dark saucers and always blinking, so he doesn't give away much. I paw at the loose dirt a little and say, "You've never said one word to that boy. He wouldn't believe a thing you said."

The mule laughs. "First time for everything."

"You're bluffing. It was dark. And I don't think you could see anything from the stable."

"Perhaps," he says. "But you see? Now I know you are a horrible liar. And I just noticed you have flecks of chicken blood all over your nose."

I lick my nose. Sure enough, it tastes like dirt and chicken blood.

Fuck.

"This is what I want," Gus says. "I stay silent about the chicken, and in return you find a way to get me out of here. Out the gate. Out into the world."

"You wouldn't last ten minutes out there," I say. "And how do you think I'm going to slip a whole mule through the gate, in broad daylight? You don't move so fast anymore, you know."

He flicks his head again, annoyed at the flies. "That's your problem, dog. I want to be free. I want to eat wild grass before I die. I want to drink cool water from a river, not from some goddamn trough."

I have to bite my tongue to keep from laughing, because I think this mule has pulled one cart too many. He sounds like a dog, not a pack animal.

"Figure it out," Gus says. "Or else, who knows, the Kid might find out about the case of the wandering chicken, and then you lose a best friend." He turns to go, but stops. "Now, promise me. Give me your word."

"Promise you what?"

"Promise me you'll get me out of here. A dog keeps his word, right? Dogs have *rules*, isn't that what you're always bragging about?"

Out of the corner of my eye, I watch Kid turn around to look at us; he's wondering what's keeping me. "All right, mule," I grumble. "I promise."

"Good," the mule says, turning back to the stable. "Now get rid of the evidence on your snout. And get to work."

I roll in the dirt for a few seconds, then catch up to the Kid and we walk together towards the gate. I had no idea Gus could talk like that. And for a mule, he's pretty damn good at blackmail, too.

These humans blow this whole dragon thing out of proportion. Listen, I've never seen one slimy scale or even smelled one whiff of this dragon since I've been here, so it could just be another story. Even if it came right up to me and breathed sour dragon breath right on my head, I don't see what all the fuss is about. I mean, it's a *beast*. Big deal. It's got fangs, we got fangs. It's got claws, we got claws, too. And whenever I look over Kid's shoulder at the old picture books in the bottom of Carnegie and he comes to a part with dragons, the pictures always show them getting stabbed to death by somebody. Sure, they're huge, probably bigger than the biggest yak ever to walk the earth, even. And sure, I hear they even breathe fire. But a beast is a beast, and I'm guessing dragons got a jugular just like everybody else—okay, everything besides chickens—and if I ever do meet this dragon in some dark arroyo, I'll know just what to do.

I won't get my hopes up. It's probably not even real, this dragon. Humans lie worse than hyenas sometimes, like the time they got me all excited because they listened to something called Three Dog Night on the doo-hickey: listen, there was not one single dog on there, not one bark. And the more I learn about history and Texas and the way the world used to be, the more I'm sure humans liked to make up stories just to scare other humans. In Texas, there was supposed to be an ugly human named Boogie Man who hid under beds and scared the shit out of kids in the night; but when a dog digs a little deeper, turns out no one here had actually seen this man, or smelled him with their own nose. That's how I feel about this dragon: it might only be a Boogie Dragon, a story made up by the older humans of Armageddon to keep people away from these mountains for some reason or another. Maybe this works on the Kid, but I am a dog, and I am not scared by silly stories.

But I'm ready, in case one day I do suddenly come nose to nose with a giant lizard that breathes fire. And I'm trying to get Kid ready, too—but like the humans say, you can't lick blood out of a stone. Which is actually true. Yeah, I've tried it.

Here's something else the old humans used to say: *every dog has its day.* I'm not sure exactly what this means, but I have a guess. If dogs were indeed the toughest animal in Texas, then every dog would get its own chance at being a famous dog, a great and worshipped dog, like the God but a dog instead of a human with a white beard. And as a dog, you were given this one day to prove yourself, because the next day, another dog had *their* chance to be great. And so on. I look at the storybook of Old Yeller and think *now there was a dog that had its day* and made the most of it, saving that poor kid from certain death, and paying for it with his dog life.

Of course, I guess if I'm only the dog here, maybe *every* day is my day.

At the end of the world, I bet all those sick, sweater-wearing dogs of Texas let their days pass without much of a fight. The days came and went. I wonder if humans each had their own day of reckoning, too? Or was it just dogs? *Every human has his day.*

No, that just doesn't sound right.

When my dog-day comes, I think I'll just know it. When I dream on my dog-bed, I always picture a standoff in the wilderness: this salty dog pitted against some yak-sized creature from Hell that looks down at me and thinks, *oh well, I've got another puny animal cornered.* Little does he know! Oh sure, we'll probably circle each other a few times, and there'll be a lot of growling and licking of chops. And then—well, then comes the moment of truth where we see what is *beast*, and what is *prey*.

It's another boring morning. Kid and me get an early start and head out to our favorite spot on the river. Today I'm trying to teach him how to corner his prey and move in for the kill. It's not easy, but at least this time he's got his knife in his paw, instead of tucked inside his trousers. There's a wiry little lizard about the length of my front leg, and he's backed up against a big rock. The lizard turns purple when it is frightened, but right now it's only a light green, so I scowl at the thing, to remind it.

What the Kid doesn't know is, I already worked out a deal with this lizard to act cornered and afraid, to boost the Kid's confidence. In return it gets a lifetime pass from being eaten by the dog. I didn't know when I made the deal that lizards are fast, but they are horrible actors.

"That's it, Kid! That's it!" I bark over to him. "Side to side,

side to side, just like I showed you. Remember the rules: corner left, corner right, and *then* pounce."

But as soon as the Kid gets close enough to strike, he stops cold in his tracks. The lizard doesn't need an invitation, it flickers away in the red dust; it even sticks its tongue out at me before it disappears under the rock. I am seriously thinking about going back on the whole *Dogs have rules* thing when the boy turns away and looks longingly at the river.

I come closer, rubbing my nose against his leg. "Good form. You were so close."

The Kid sits down on a flat rock and sinks his head down between his hind legs. "I do not think I could kill something that could also be my friend."

"You're thinking like a human. You need to think more like a dog. Take me, for instance. I can eat other animals I know, anytime." This is mostly a lie, and I barely knew that chicken, but hey, I'm trying to get a boy ready to fight a dragon here.

He looks up with a sad face. "So you could eat me?"

I think about it. "I guess I could," I say. "If I was very hungry, and we were no longer best friends."

The Kid smiles. "We will always be best friends."

I rest the pad of my paw on his front leg. "Then I'll never eat you."

He laughs. "You could not eat me anyway, Dog. Your jaws are too small."

"Funny," I say, licking my chops as I stare at his front leg like it is a chicken. "Say that to me again, and they'll start calling you Lefty." This was, of course, a joke. Kid is my best friend and he knows my weaknesses: dogs are not vain creatures, at least not as vain as the pigs and wading birds, but we do have two things we take very seriously: the size of our jaws, and the smell of our fur. If you want to insult a dog, make a crack about their fangs being dull. Just watch your back after you say it.

Kid jumps up, pretending like he's about to corner me like the lizard. Yeah, right. One thing is for sure: this baby human is going to get a fish in his trousers very soon.

We're about to head back to Armagdeddon when I pick up a faint sound coming from behind us with my dog ears, a kind of shrill whistle. After a few moments, Kid starts to hear it too, and we both turn to stare down the river, towards the direction of the sea. For a while, we don't see anything. Then in the distance, we both see a glint of silver light on the water, something square reflecting the sunlight. Then two squares, and then three. Kid shields his eyes with his hand, trying to get a better look. "Ben has returned," he yells, dropping the knife in the dust and breaking into a run.

"You dropped your knife in the dust," I say after him, but he is already too far down the riverbank to hear. The boy has a lot to learn. I sniff at the rock and whisper to the lizard underneath it that he is one lucky lizard, and then I catch up to Kid. We watch the yellow sky as the boats slide up the river towards us.

"They are missing one boat," the boy says. I tell him I can count, too.

When they land in the shallows and start to unload their boats, I also notice they have brought back an alien creature from across the sea.

Much later, when we are back inside Armageddon, I find out this is called a *girl*.

From our favorite spot on the river, I watch Kid walk right up to the girl; from this distance I think they're almost identical standing next to each other, besides their clothes: the same black mangy fur on top of their round heads, the same size, the same skinny hind legs, the same big, dark eyes like mules. They are talking about something. When I come closer they talk in a whisper, like they have secrets, even though they just met.

"This is Dog," Kid says, pointing over to me. "He's a dog."

"What's a dog?" the girl says, looking at me strangely, like I'm the one who just stepped off a boat, not her.

What's a dog? Who's never heard of a dog?

I sit back and raise a paw in friendship, barking sweetly. "We're best friends, the Kid and me."

But all she does is hold her nose and walks away. "He smells funny," she says, then walks right past me in the direction of Armageddon. I growl—*he smells funny?*—but Kid follows behind her like a puppy, taking some of Ben's gear along on his back as he goes. I get the feeling he is not coming back. I stand my ground by the river, wondering what I smell like, besides dog. Maybe it's still that damned chicken.

"Hey, Kid," I yell after him. "What about trying to swim the river? There's still daylight. Perfect time to avoid being eaten." I realize this is what humans call *desperate*. I throw in a few pants and a tail wag; hell, even if I have to finally break down and hump a leg out here to get some attention, I'm going to do it.

Some of the fighting men that belong to Ben pass by from the boats with heavy packs, heading towards Armageddon. The one called Smokey pats my head as he walks past. "Good dog," he says to me. "Good dog." Suddenly it's colder out here and my whole body shivers like I need to shake water off my fur, even though I'm dry. It feels weird, standing here alone. It feels like someone has just stolen my best friend—and then I realize, that's exactly what happened.

When dogs dream, we dream in packs. From what I can tell, a dog dream looks a lot like any human dream: endless meadows, deep forests, wide lakes and streams to paddle across, and back again. But the difference is, our dreams always have other dogs in them. For dogs, paradise is something that always has to be shared. For us, hell is being alone. When I listen to the humans talk about their dreams around the fire at night, they always seem to be picturing paradise as being on their own. What kind of dreams are these? Who wants to find their own way out of a nightmare, without any help? This, I'll never understand. When dogs dream, we dream in packs. And when we die, we die together.

It's yet another morning, but today is different because it's way past dawn and I still have not seen a sign of the Kid anywhere. I look like a dummy, waiting alone outside the Carnegie. I can hear the chickens scratching around their yard, already spreading their gossip. But I'm worried because Kid is always the first to arrive, and for the first time he's not here.

The sun is already over the walls when he finally comes towards the front of Carnegie from Cookie's place. He has that girl with him. "Good morning, Dog," he says, like nothing is wrong. She does not say anything. "We are going to detect some poetry books in the basement of Carnegie, and read some poems to each other."

This must be another joke. "But you hate poetry." I laugh, but I am the only one. "Forget poetry. Let's go to the river like we always do, and we can finish that lizard for good."

"We might go out there later," he says, and when he says *we* he does not mean Kid and Dog. He means Kid and this alien girl. Suddenly he is talking to me like we're not in the same pack. "I want to show Eve around first."

"But what about the counting? And the mysteries. We've got a lot of work to do. We have at least three mysteries to solve."

"What is the dog talking about?" the girl says. I realize she speaks dog, too. "Mysteries?"

"Oh, it's nothing," Kid says, coughing like he is suddenly sick. "Listen, Dog, I will observe you later."

This is what I want to say to him: *the hell you will*. But

instead I say, "Sure." Yeah, I do exactly what dogs are expected to do in this situation: I lick the Kid's hand a couple times, and then I turn away. I hear the chickens snicker to each other as I pad across the farmyard towards my dog bed next to Tiny's butcher shop. It's still morning but I slide onto my soft bed made of old hemp and rest my head on the edge. I'm supposed to be working, but I don't feel like it.

Right now I feel like staying here, and not moving for a long, long while.

I close my eyes and remember another thing the humans always say about the dogs of Texas: *let sleeping dogs lie*. And I never knew what that meant, until just now.

The sun falls a few more times before I get wise and stop waiting for the Kid at the steps of Carnegie each morning. Now I figure my pack is down to one. I haven't forgotten about my promise to the damn mule, though; even a lone dog keeps his word. So one night, when the moon is high and I know all the humans are sleeping, I slip out to the stables and growl a little by the fence. The mule is already there, waiting in the shadows. I tell him, *conditions are perfect*. He nods and kicks out a loose board with his hind legs and together we sneak over to the gate. Mule hides behind the wall of Carnegie while I scratch my front paws against their noisy metal gate a few times, finally getting the human above gate to look down. When he sees me in his torchlight, I bark loudly over and over. This human called Smokey looks at me with concern, and I know I have him. "What's wrong, Dog?"

I can understand humans perfectly, but I do not speak their language. So I bark some more, turn in a circle and then throw in a couple of points towards the outside of the wall, which should seal the deal. Humans are not the smartest creatures, but if you bark long enough at them, sooner or later they can figure it out on their own. Plus, their hearing sucks.

"Hey, I think he's trying to tell us the Kid's gone over," Smokey says to the other human in the watch tower, both of them now searching the horizon. "Open the fucking gate, and let's take a look."

Perfect. I give the mule a signal, and he trots out from his hiding place. He says, "Well, Dog, you kept your word."

I smell around. "You'd better hurry, they won't leave the gate for long."

"You could come with me," the mule says. "I could use a set of fangs on my side."

I laugh at this. "Go with you? Listen, I can come and go whenever I please."

Then he turns his big fat mule head back towards Carnegie. "Are you sure about that?"

I am becoming hot under my fur because inside, I know he is right. I've been talking about following my dog instincts for as long as I remember, and here's a chance to do it, and I'm wavering. This is not the way for the first dog in the world to act, I tell myself.

The mule turns to slip out the gate, disappearing into the dark beyond.

And what do I do?

I bare my teeth, and I do what the first dog was born to do: I run. I *roam*.

We know we are lost when we run as far as the river, but the river's not there. Somehow we have gone the wrong way; in the darkness and excitement, we must have gone in the opposite direction, because nothing here smells familiar to me. I tell myself this is a good thing, since this means we are *wild*. We are following our own path. It means we are officially roaming. I tell this to Gus, too, but the mule is suddenly not much on conversation again. He doesn't say anything, he's too busy breathing hard, his sloppy tongue hanging out of his mouth.

I've already learned one important rule in the short time I've spent escaping with the mule: never escape with a mule. They are stubborn, and they need a lot of water. And you can't let a mule take the lead, because they shit while they walk—really, they do!—and if you're stuck behind that, well—watch your step.

But I am the leader of this pack now. Suddenly, something smells wrong. "Hold on, mule," I say, sniffing the red dust. I know the smell of death when I smell it. And right now, I smell it. "We're heading towards the Graveyard," I tell him. "We need to turn around."

"*Wrong.* I can smell the river ahead," he says, breathing

hard through his nostrils. "It's this way, all right." His voice is shaky; I can tell he's already wishing he was standing in front of a nice trough right about now. Truth be told, I wouldn't mind my nice round bowl myself.

I turn back and nip at his haunch as he limps along in the darkness. "You're going to die of thirst soon if we don't head back."

But he kicks at me, missing badly. "Who made you leader? You want to go back, go ahead. I'm going this way, where there's water."

I am about to just let him go and die his mule death, but suddenly there is a piercing shriek that splits the air. Then another. Mule and I both look at each other, frozen in our tracks. It sounds like the shrill calls of the flying beasts that Hyatt calls Telemarketers, which is not good. We must be closer to the Graveyard than I thought.

The mule backs up a hoof. "I think we went the wrong way."

"No shit." I lower my voice to a whisper. "Listen, whatever you do, *don't run*. Stand your—" but before I can even finish, Gus has turned and started into full gallop in the opposite direction. The *clop-clop-clop* is about as noisy as paws can get. What's worse is this: in the dark, he thinks he is running in a straight line, but I can see he's just circling back to where I am, exactly like the chicken in the farmyard. He is going in a big circle, round and round. What is it about farm animals running in circles? When the mule orbits the second time in his panic, he stops and says, "How did you get here so fast?"

The shrieks are louder now. I tell the mule to shut up and get behind me.

Peering into the night, I feel a rush of air cross the hairs of my face. It's here, all right. In an instant I see it, dropping down from the sky right in front of me, taller than a human and with jet black wings flapping at us. It growls at me, but this salty dog growls right back. We can't run. I figure if this is the last stand of the world's first dog, then hell, it's going to be a good one. This monster takes a step towards me with its crooked bird foot. I put a paw forward too. This thing laughs; I get it, he's expecting me to run away, like the mule, so he can chase us both down.

But I am a dog, and dogs do the chasing.

I tell myself, if anyone is going to whimper and beg for its life, it's sure as hell not going to be me. I stare into this thing's cold, black eyes and I say in my head, *you picked on the wrong dog tonight. This is not the kind of dog that wears sweaters and hats, oh no. This is the kind of dog that used to live in a junkyard. This is the first dog, and he is going to beat your fucking ass.*

The thing shrieks again and lunges towards me with its huge vulture-beak wide open, but on the ground it moves too slow and I leap to one side as it lumbers past. Before it can turn around to face me again I am already on its neck, going for the jugular. I don't really think about it, I just do it. In a moment my teeth are sunk in deep down to the gums and I hold on for life while this beast thrashes around, flailing its sharp claws in the air, raking at the fur of my back.

But I do not let go. Now I can feel its warm blood trickling past my tongue. The blood is spilling out of its throat, and I can feel this creature start to weaken under me, slowing down and bending to the ground. The shrieking is only a gurgle now. I keep ripping my jaws back and forth, like a wolf would do, until we're on the ground and finally this thing stops moving. I look around quickly, ready for another one to attack, but I realize am alone. The mule has disappeared; maybe he tried to run in a circle and ended up back at Armageddon. My back sears with pain from the claws of this beast, and I am dizzy, but I lick the blood off my paw, and I taste the bits of flesh left in my mouth. God, it tastes good. I can feel my own blood matting the fur of my back. I try to walk but after only a few woozy steps I fall down. I'm smiling, at least. The night around me is silent as I lie next to this dead thing from Disneyland. We will probably die together.

I close my eyes and say to him: *Tonight, I am the hunter.* I laugh and whisper at its cold ear: *Tonight, motherfucker, I am the beast.*

This is how I know I'm not dead: I hear the mule telling lies. He is telling Kid and the girl how he had fought off at least four winged demons, one demon for each hoof, while I slinked into safety to lick my wounds. "There I was," Gus the mule says. "Deep in the Graveyard, protecting my friend, Dog."

I hear the girl suck in her breath. "Were you scared?"

"Scared?" The mule snorts back. "Horses get scared, honey. I'm a mule."

I open my crusty eyes into bright sunlight and drag my tongue along my dry chops. I'm lying in my own bed made of plants, but for some reason I cannot move anything below my neck. I see Kid leaning on the fence post by the stables, slicing a piece of fruit to feed the mule. I look down at my body and immediately coil in horror: I am wrapped in something fluffy that has ugly patterns of red and blue, patterns I have seen before in the books of Carnegie.

"This looks like a fucking sweater," I say, baring my teeth. I try to bite at it, but I can barely move my neck.

Kid runs over to me from the fence. "Stop that, Dog. Listen, it's not a sweater, it's a blanket. Evangeline made it just for you."

"You are trying to make me wear a sweater before I die," I say.

The girl he calls Evangeline comes closer. "You don't wear it, silly. You lie on it when you sleep. It's made of Alabama cotton, and it's soft, see?" She lifts a corner of it against my nose and it feels very soft, like chicken feathers, only less itchy.

Truth be told, it kind of feels wonderful.

"So you speak dog, too," I say to her. "Like the Kid."

She nods. "Always been able to, I guess."

I am very tired still, and I start to yawn. Tomorrow, I will try to get up and walk around, test my aching bones. But today, I will sleep. Tonight, I know I will dream of my dog pack crossing the wilderness together, singing at our silent moon, like a real Three Dog Night.

Dogs dream in packs, after all. And tonight, we dream of yak.

IV.
Two Great Lights

So this was what was left of Texas: one half swallowed by the sea, the other half buried under a desert. He hadn't been back since the War. There were no landmarks anymore, at least none he could recognize. But he knew he was getting close, close enough to smell them both in the lazy, passing breeze.

He kicked out the stand on his dusty bike with his boot heel and stood up from the saddle, trying to stretch his aching back. He shook out his legs, slapping some of the dust from his worn chaps. Riding this fatboy was a whole lot easier back when there were roads, he thought to himself. It probably wasn't the most low-profile way to travel, but who cared about appearances now? *Fuck low-profile*, he thought. He was still an Angel, which was about as high-profile as it got. He was still the Darkness. And he would become the Serpent once again, to get what he wanted. But right now, as the hot wind smacked his face, this motorcycle was still the closest he could come to flying again.

Not for long, he muttered, his eyes searching the empty sky. *Not for long.*

To the west, he could feel a change in the weather. Yes, another two or three days' ride and he'd be right back where everything had ended: that graveyard of souls that people still called Armageddon, the same place where it was all about to begin again. What was the old lie that little bastard Sam told his lost sheep, when he was alive? *The last shall be first, and the first shall be last.* The rider spit into the dust and shook his ragged head. All lies. Maybe it was fitting, he thought: the last story ever told in that dying world was an utter lie.

He had overheard the stories people had told about a few lost sheep living in a walled town named Armageddon. They had even managed to find themselves some kind of *hero*. The orphans he'd left behind on the battlefield were no doubt keeping this hero busy; they were his own lost children, squalling beasts left behind to wander the wasteland. An accounting error, the rider smirked. *This was never an exact science*, he mumbled as he shrugged his broad shoulders and tugged at his grizzled grey beard.

It would be good to see those old comrades again.

And now, after these thirty years of wandering, he would be able to give them brand new orders: find me this boy, and this girl. Bring them to me, alive.

The travelers stayed close to their wagons as they waited outside the gates of Armageddon, drinking from their water sacks that were fat now from crossing the river. There were five of them, all old men born long before the War, each staring west in silent wonder as a dark bloom of purple clouds billowed up on the far horizon, as if the mountains had caught fire. Even from a distance these men knew they were not clouds at all, but a warning; they could feel a sharp wind blowing east across the open desert, pressing their rough faces. And yet these clouds did not move. Overhead, a ragged flock of black cormorants suddenly buzzed their wagons, riding the hot wind towards the sea, screeching back and forth in a hasty language of escape.

The travelers nodded to one another with grim faces. They did not have to say out loud what they already knew in their dry bones: something was coming.

There had been signs. On their slow journey north through the rocky strip of Old Mexico, they had watched the faded moon inch higher in the midday sky; a few more days, maybe a week, and there would be an eclipse, turning the world to black. And then there was the silence: three days ago they had crossed the wide wash of the Pishon River to the south, and they had not heard the screams and sad cries they had expected. It was as if the leftover creatures from Hell had all vanished through a trapdoor, or worse, lay in hiding somewhere out of sight. In some ways, the silence had been more frightening than those horrible voices of the night, making sleep impossible.

And now, this sinister eruption of clouds behind Mount Megiddo. Something was coming, it was clear: even the cormorants had heard the story of the dragon that still lived in the mountain that loomed over Armageddon.

Four of the men craned their necks to follow the birds as they dissolved in the distance until they were only black dots dancing on the lemon-colored sky. Their leader sat by himself in the lead wagon, a wire-thin man who leaned both his hands patiently on a gnarled cane made of whale bone. He was working a slice of peyote under his tired gums; once in a while he leaned over and spat juice to the ground. One of the other men had put a metal cup of water on the bench beside him, but he had not touched it. Somehow a line from an old movie lingered in his memory: *when I drink water, I drink water, and when I drink whiskey, I drink whiskey.* Or in this case, *peyote.* It was funny how memory worked: he could remember some random line from a John Wayne film he'd seen as a kid, but he couldn't remember things like his older sister Martha's face, or the sound of his younger sister's voice as she'd call his name out like a curse.

Or even what it felt like to wake up and rise from the dead.

He sat patiently, watching the horizon; they had passed a funeral cortege at the river crossing, so he knew there would be a long wait. No doubt his old friend Hyatt was among them, saying goodbye to today's lucky dead.

I don't feel old, he said to himself, listening to his own raspy breath, feeling the thump of his heart in his throat.

But whenever he saw his reflection in a mirror—they had several tucked in the wagons for trade—he saw the deep grooves around his mouth and eyes and the dark patches of skin on his cheeks and they reminded him he'd lived more than one life.

In his previous life, he'd drowned to death, only to be brought back to life. He wasn't the only man still alive who called the dead lucky, but he was the only one on earth who knew it was true.

Yes, he thought as he sat still and waited. They were all lucky, the dead.

"Welcome back, Queen," Hyatt's voice called from behind him. Queen: it was a name he'd given himself after the War, a name that used to have *irony*, back when irony meant something in the world. Now it was just a name like any other.

"*Bonjour*," he said, extending a withered hand into the air. "My old friend. We ask for shelter for the night, and in the morning we will be able to trade some things you may need."

Hyatt leaned a leg on the wagon and squinted. "Got anything good? Tell the truth."

Queen coughed. "Now what kind of salesman would I be if I told you the truth?"

"You got me there." Hyatt looked the wagons over. "You seem to be down to five. Last time you were here, there must've been a dozen."

"And before that, maybe twenty of us. Sooner or later we'll be down to one and I'll be pulling the wagons myself."

He reached out one hand and Hyatt helped him down from the wooden seat. "We saw you saying goodbye to some of your own on the way in."

"Yeah, another one of Ben's crew. We're down to about twenty-three ourselves."

Queen leaned on the side of the wagon, his legs still not ready for walking. "Old age?"

Hyatt nodded. "Yeah, the lucky bastard. Only way I want to go."

"Amen to that," Queen said, slipping his hand inside his robe and pulled out a small leather pouch, offering it to his friend. "A gift from the deserts of Old Mexico?"

"Don't mind if I do," Hyatt said, nodding wearily. He took out a flat piece of peyote and slid it into his mouth. "We're still going to have to search you and your crew for weapons," he said, spitting into the dust. "You know the drill, amigo. Can't be too careful, you know."

"No one searches travelers but travelers," Queen said, standing up to his full height.

"Have it your way, old buddy," Hyatt sighed. They had been through this same dance before, maybe a half-dozen times now. "Gets pretty dangerous out here for humans when that sun goes down, though."

Queen looked at him with keen eyes. "Luckily, I consider you a brother, Hyatt, which means we're both travelers. Search away."

Hyatt put a hand on his heart. "I'm honored, as long as we don't have to swap blood or fuck the same goat. Okay,

Smokey," Hyatt yelled impatiently up to the tower, twirling his hand in the air. The travelers climbed on to the wagons, talking to the oxen.

"Those clouds," Queen said as he followed behind Hyatt on foot. "Behind the mountains. I do not remember anything like that, last time we passed through here."

"Yeah, we got some strange things going on around here, all right. Must be close to Halloween or some shit."

"Is Ben Wolf here?"

Hyatt paused. "Uh, I think he's out on another mission or something, I'm not sure."

"You're not sure? I thought Navy Seals didn't do anything without a plan."

Hyatt stopped and turned around. "Been a long time since anyone's called him that."

"Yes, I guess the old names don't work these days. What did it say on your driver's license, back in the day? Mister Hyatt G. Lacy? From ... Londonderry, Northern Ireland?"

"Sure, Queen," Hyatt said, clearly annoyed. "And for the record, it was just *Derry*." He walked backwards, waving the wagon drivers into the open gates of Armageddon. "I guess it would sound strange if I called you *Lazlo Hooker*. All the way from good old North Dakota, U.S.A."

Lazlo Hooker. Now there was a name that had risen from the dead.

They were sitting on the edge of the water a few feet apart from one another, their toes dug deep into the cool mud of the riverbank. A weird storm had been churning behind Mount Megiddo for days, and now the water that flowed past them in the River Gihon was high and cold. Dog was downstream, busy chasing a purple lizard in and out of the thick shocks of green sawgrass that choked the shore at the deep bend of the river.

Sitting cross-legged on a flat rock, Kid glanced up from his notebook now and then to stare at the girl. She was writing in her notebook, too, but from a distance it didn't look like writing at all. To the boy, it kind of looked like a big mess: she had drawn sloppy pictures without any words to explain them, and there were tons of crazy scribbles and patterns that wasted whole pages. And he noticed that when she did write words, they didn't always go left to right; sometimes they didn't even go all the way across the page, like they were supposed to in a proper book. The boy could only shake his head at the shambles. This girl obviously had never heard of important English words like *paragraph* and *sentence*.

Sometimes she wrote her words straight up and down the page, or diagonally, or in crazy loops and spirals, or curved around the corners, like the words were all fireflies trapped in a jar. Her letters went from big to small to big again. Sometimes he'd watch her write and it looked like she was stabbing her notebook to death with the pencil, trying to murder each page. Every page in her notebook looked completely different from the others. Where was the order, the logic? *What a waste*, he thought again. He felt sorry for her, because it was obvious no one in Alabama had taught her any of the rules.

After staring at her for a while, the Kid went back to the list he was writing. Soon Eve started to hum a song to herself, lifting her feet out of the mud to paddle them in the shallow water, making a racket.

"You do not want to splash too much," he warned. "You do not want to be eaten."

"Yeah, you mentioned that," she said, still paddling. "Thanks for the tip."

As she splashed, Eve watched Dog out of the corner of her eye, waiting until he was out of earshot, even for his dog ears. Then she took a deep breath and leaned over to Kid. "I'm running away tomorrow," she whispered. "Just so you know."

He put his notebook down. "I do not understand."

"*I'm running away tomorrow,*" she repeated, louder this time. She watched Dog perk his ears up for a moment, before heading back to the hunt. She lowered her voice again. "Like your storybooks in Carnegie. The children always run away for a while." She turned a page back to her notebook, flipping to a new page. "You can come along if you want. I guess I could use someone good with maps."

The Kid snorted. "If you cannot read a map, you will become lost."

"Maybe that's the point," she said. "Maybe I don't want to know where I'm going."

"That makes no sense, Evangeline."

"Yeah, well," she said. "Maybe that's my middle name, *No Sense.*"

He flipped back a few pages to find his list of things to call The Girl and wrote this down, right below Evangeline. "Why did you choose the name Evangeline?"

She tilted her head back a little and smiled, saying the name to herself a couple times. "I just liked the sound of it. And it's got *angel* right in the middle."

He scratched at his bushy hair. "That does not make sense, either."

She turned to him. "Listen, it's not *supposed* to make sense," she said, dropping her book into her lap to shake her arms above her head. "It's supposed to make me feel good." As she faced the river again, she could hear him go back to his writing. Then there was a silence between them, making her think she'd hurt him. So she said, "And what about you? I can't go on calling you Kid forever, you know."

He chewed his lip as he thought about it. "Do I get to choose?"

"I did," Eve giggled. "If we're not going to name things around here, then who will?"

The Kid looked up into the sky. "Well, Hyatt once stated I reminded him of a hero in a story he observed as a child."

Her whole body shook. "Please stop saying *state* all the time. There's a lot of other words you can use, you know. And while you're at it, ditch *observe* too. Those words sound so cold to me when you say them. It's like you're writing a history book or something. "

He held up his notebook. "But I am writing a history book."

"Oh," she said. She turned her head away so only the fish in the river could see her stick out her tongue, like she'd just bit into a lemon. "Yeah, sorry."

After a moment, his head popped up again. "Why do the fish say you are sick?"

She mumbled some French words under her breath. Sometimes she forgot they could both speak all the same languages; back in Alabama she'd gotten used to having secret conversations with the fish, the birds, and the wild cats that roamed the forest at night. "So, what was the name Hyatt gave you?" she said, eager to change the subject. "From the old television show, I mean."

"It is stupid," he said, laughing. "Accordion to Hyatt, there was a man named Commander Adamma who was the hero of the story. He was the leader, and he read many books. So Hyatt called me *Adamma*."

Now she was laughing along with him. "You're right, Commander," she said. "That *is* stupid. Sounds too much like *drama*. Still, it's a lot better than Kid. Maybe you could shorten it a little, so it sounds less like *Mama*." She wrote the name down a few times on the margins of the page, in different variations. "Tell you what, I'll just call you *Adam*."

He said it to himself a few times under his breath. It sounded good, simple. "Have you decided where you will run away tomorrow?"

She closed her eyes, putting her notebook down on the flat rock beside her. "No, I don't know. That's the whole point," she said, standing up. "You're running *away*. You're not running *to*. You're not supposed to know where you're going. You make it up as you go. That's the fun of it."

"That does not sound like fun," he said, making a face. "That sounds like a mystery."

"Exactly," she said. "I'm pretty sure they're the same thing." She slipped her feet out of the slick river mud and stretched her thin legs slowly like some kind of elegant wading bird. "And do me one more favor, Adam," she said, folding her arms on her chest. "When you get back to Carnegie, look up *accordion* in that big dictionary of yours. I got a feeling you're using it wrong."

Dog trotted up to where they were sitting. "Someone's running?"

"Um, yeah," the girl said, thinking fast. She pointed to the river. "It's the fish. See? They're running pretty fast. Something must be spooking them."

Dog shook off a water chill. "Fish don't know anything," he said, lapping up some water with his tongue. "Sometimes I think they're even dumber than the chickens." He peered into the river, watching the shadows move along the shallow bottom. "But they *are* running pretty fast downstream, though."

"They are definitely scared about something," the boy said. "But they say they do not know what, exactly. It's just their instincts, I guess. I mean, they just *know*."

Dog looked up. "So is that why you're running away to-morrow?"

She bit her lip. "So you *did* hear?"

Dog nodded, and perked up his ears. "Hey, I'm a dog." Suddenly, a low rumble echoed across the desert from the mountains. It sounded like a distant roar, and they all fell silent and looked west, half-expecting to see a dragon rise out of the smoke that lingered above Mount Megiddo like a phoenix. But it was only the low rumble of thunder; they saw jagged flashes of lightning bursting against the dark curtain of clouds. Dog picked up something in the hot wind that he had not smelled before, and it made him bark. Then the three of them sat perfectly still for a while and watched the tiny white bolts dance above the mountain tops in the distance. Soon another blast of thunder rolled past them towards the open sea.

"Okay, maybe I was wrong about the fish," Dog whispered.

As dusk approached Armageddon, the old men and women gathered in the wide clearing between the gate and Carnegie, lighting up their pipes and passing around the last of the corn wine. The travelers had built a bonfire from one of their gutted wagons; it was an easy sacrifice to make, Queen had announced, when there would soon be more wagons than men. They had brought out fresh clumps of the green peyote from Old Mexico and brewed their hosts strong coffee from further south; as the sky bled into deep indigo, everyone in the lopsided circle passed along whatever came into their hands: huge joints rolled in flat sawgrass from the river, clay water bowls, cups of the Alabama wine, plates heaped with toasted hemp seed. There was laughter, and for a moment they all could be forgiven for thinking they were at some happy memory from a different world, a holiday picnic or scout jamboree. Cookie was sitting beside one of the strangers and humming a broken tune, trying to remember the words of an old country song that the traveler only knew the first line to.

Queen sat facing the old granite library, his back propped up against a pile of stacked pillows and hemp blankets. Hyatt reclined near him, leaning against his elbow in the dirt, his red eyes bleary with smoke and perhaps too much wine. Queen looked around the circle with a faint smile, listening to bits of all the voices flying back and forth around him. "Do you remember when people used to say conversation was a lost art?"

"Yeah," Hyatt said. "Fucking *computers*. Fucking *texting*. What a world that was."

Queen nodded. "That's irony for you. Now conversation is the only art we've got left." His head was clear. He had been trying not to stare at the boy and the girl who were sitting on the steps of Carnegie, a stone's throw away, There was a dog at the children's feet, finishing its dinner in a bowl.

Across the clearing, the boy and the girl sat on the steps of Carnegie, notebooks propped in their laps. The orange glow from the bonfire shed just enough light for them to see what they were writing. They were listening to all the conversations going on around the fire and furiously writing down all the words they hadn't heard before. It was all new to them, another new language to learn from the past. From their dusty memories, the old people talked about their favorite foods from Texas: peanut butter, Nutter Butters, Pearl Jam, espresso, collard greens. They talked about their favorite histories on the television, like Columbo, Steve McQueen; the New York Jets, the Blair Witch Project, Breaking Bad. The old people became somber when they began to reminisce about the great tragedies of history: a spaceship called Challenger, a day called Nine-Eleven and a group called Van Halen, with and without a man named David Lee Roth. None of this was in the history books of Carnegie, and both the boy and the girl savored the secrets they were gleaning. As the night wore on, the old people started to talk more about sex: there were stories of a dead man named Ron Jeremy, another about someone named Dirty Sanchez, and at least three about a crazy woman named Reverse Cowgirl.

Eve looked up from her writing for a moment, puzzled. "Reverse cowgirl?"

"Don't worry, I already know her story," Adam said. "I will tell you later."

After a while, the conversations between the old people started to die down a little as they all passed things between each other. "We'll leave early tomorrow, like usual, only we won't tell them we're not coming back." "We'll head towards the river, see how far we get."

"In English that was called *south*," he said. "The direction towards the river, I mean."

"Thanks for the geography," she said, rolling her eyes. "Are you still coming?"

He looked around first, then nodded.

"Good. I was thinking, we'll need supplies. Maybe Hyatt has some things we can use in his workshop."

"No one's allowed in there. Not even I have seen inside his workshop."

She shrugged her shoulders. "Okay. You're the one good at lists. Make us a list of things we'll need when we run away."

He looked up, thinking hard; after a few moments he hunched over his notebook again. He liked the idea that he was being useful to her. "We'll need food. And I know where we can get hemp sacks to carry everything. Oh, and Dog," he said. His friend lifted his heavy head in recognition. "Can we take your blanket?"

"Sure, as long as I'm coming," Dog yawned. "I do have some experience in running away, you know." He lowered his head again, closing his tired eyes.

"Oh, great," Eve said. "Who else is tagging along? The chickens? Why not the mule, too?"

"Trust me," Dog said lazily. "You don't ever want to run away with a mule."

"Do not worry. It will just be the three of us," Adam said. "Just like the record of the Three Musketeers, by Alexandre Dumas." He went back to his list-making. "I will try to borrow Ben's compass in the morning."

The girl looked over at him with a frown. "What's a compass?"

He did not look up. "It is a device that shows you the direction you are going."

"Fuck that," she said, turning away. "I told you, I don't want to know where I'm going."

Now it was the boy wearing the frown. "But—"

Instantly, she reached out and covered his mouth with the palm of her hand. "Listen, if you say *it makes no sense* one more time, I'm going to punch you."

Now the bonfire had sagged into a bed of coals now, glowing red in the darkness. The wood from the wagon was just about spent, just a few shards left. One of the travelers stood up, wobbly from too much wine, and tossed the last bit of a wheel into the fiery circle. In a few seconds it sparked into black smoke, thick flames licking up into the night air. Someone else had to push it out before the whole compound filled with the putrid fumes of burning rubber.

Hyatt and Laz were hunkered down, their heads propped up by blankets. They were still sober enough to talk business. Hyatt drained his cup of the Alabama wine and tossed it at the fire. "All right, old buddy. Down to business. You got any fulminate of mercury?"

Laz almost spit out a sip of wine. "Are you planning on blowing up a mountain?"

"Okay, okay," Hyatt said, rubbing his withered chin. "How about a crankshaft for a late model pickup?"

A smile spread slowly across Laz's face. "Now that, I might have."

"And a distributor cap while you're at it." Hyatt wagged his finger. "One that *works*, this time."

Laz nodded. "I see you're still working on your hobby, then?"

Hyatt didn't answer right away. He sat there for a minute, content to be silent, looking thoughtfully over at the steps of Carnegie, where the boy and girl sat talking to one another. Finally, he turned to Laz. "Man's got to do something with all this free time, don't he?"

Laz pushed his weathered fist into Hyatt's shoulder. "So, old friend, are you going to dodge my questions about that boy and girl all night?"

"Yeah, pretty much."

"Now, I thought there wasn't anyone born after the War."

"I thought that, too."

"But *lo and behold*, here you have a bonafide boy and girl, sitting right over there. Breathing air, right before my very eyes." The man most called Queen re-lit the joint in the folds of his tunic and took a long pull off it. "So, *mon ami*, this begs the question—"

"It don't beg nothing. Whatever question you got, answer's going to be no. And let me tell you, if Ben thinks you're even looking at one of those kids funny, he'll plant you in the ground. *Tu savais?*"

Laz whistled, like a train coming from the distance. "I thought you said Ben was away on one of his crusades."

Hyatt laughed out of the side of his mouth, coughing up something that had been deep in his throat. "Well, dipshit— you said so yourself. The guy was a Navy Seal." He stopped talking long enough to let out a loud belch. "I hear them motherfuckers can be ten places at once."

Laz only nodded in return, and fell silent, listening to the dying cacophony of ragged voices around him. Some were already preparing for sleep. He kept his stare on the steps of the library, focusing on the children's faces, their features. He wondered when the last time he'd been surprised in this life. It had been too long to remember. He felt something else he hadn't felt in a long time: *curiosity*. There would be good dreams tonight, instead of the usual nightmares.

He waited for the moon to drift behind a clutch of clouds. Suddenly he was a young Lazlo Hooker again, crawling silently through a window, his weathered hands remembering the old etiquette of breaking and entering. *This is probably the last building left standing on earth, and it's a fucking library*, he thought as he lifted his legs through, one at a time. *Good to know you still have a sense of humor, God, wherever you are.* Laz would have guessed a prison or a bank or some kind of military fortress would be the last to go, something without windows altogether. Maybe Tiffany's in New York, but he had seen New York, or what was left of it. It had reminded him of a ruined Venice, with the grid of streets turned into canals; but that was ten or twelve years ago. By now, the whole island of Manhattan was probably smoothed over completely. He'd miss it entirely if he passed it again in the night. He had seen the last bones sticking out of the ground in Chicago, Mexico City, Toronto, all names from old maps that didn't mean anything anymore. Somewhere in one of the wagons he had a green road sign from Interstates that no longer existed. The thing that had surprised him the most was how fast the world cleans itself. It had only been thirty years or so since the War, and yet the earth was already almost free of any sign of the eight billion people that once lived here. Now he had to look pretty hard for confirmation that people lived here at all. Every day he had to remind himself he used to live here, in a completely different world.

The sun would be up soon. If anyone asked what he was doing slithering into Carnegie in the dark, he wasn't sure what he would tell them; he didn't know himself. He just knew he was curious about this boy and girl. He hadn't been surprised by anything in a long time, which was saying a lot for an old man who lived in a world with a dragon in it. He didn't mean these kids any harm. He'd be content just to see one up close, to see if they were actually some trick or mirage, and maybe talk to one of them, see what secrets they held, or merely hear a voice that hadn't been worn down by time.

Inside, Laz pulled himself up from the floor and crouched against the wall. His legs and shoulders already ached from the climb. He squinted, his old eyes adjusting to the dim; the waxing moon gave him just enough light to see he was at one end of a wide corridor. He smiled as he stood up, feeling his way along the wall as he crept down the hallway. *Breaking into a library*, he mused to himself. *Yes, the boys back in James River would have loved to hear this one.*

"Hello, Queen," a voice echoed against the hard stone walls. Laz's heart skipped; the deep bellow was unmistakable. It was Ben Wolf, watching him somewhere from the darkness ahead.

Laz stood perfectly still. "Ben, my—my old friend," he said, his voice breaking. His eyes tried to search the darkness. His knees were trembling more than usual. "I was just coming to see you."

"Like Hell you were," Ben's voice called back from the dark. No emotion.

Laz wrung his hands together. "Hyatt told me you were out chasing more windmills."

Ben let out a sigh, his voice sounding a bit softer now. "Actually, I've been avoiding you." There was the scratch of flint against metal, with a spark lighting up the hallway for a split second as Ben lit a fat lamp that hung from the ceiling. Another spark, and the wick caught and slowly gave shape to the room. Ben placed the lamp on an empty shelf and came closer. In the glow, Laz could see the dour look on the hero's face.

"Listen," Ben said, motioning for Laz to sit down on a ruined chair. "When I was in Alabama, I met someone. You mentioned one time that you had a sister. *Daylene Hooker?*"

"Daylene," Laz said, confused. He hadn't said her name out loud in a long time. "You saw her? How was she?"

"Let's just say I saw her."

"Oh." For someone so good with words, that's all that came out of his mouth. From the tone of Ben's voice, Laz knew whatever had happened, it wasn't good. He thought his sister was already dead. He tried to remember the last time he saw her. Europe somewhere, before the end of everything. It was warm—yes, Italy—Florence. He remembered an echo of the last time they spoke, an argument about her boy, just a baby at the time. Sam's boy, too. "Was her son still with him?"

"They're both dead," Ben grumbled. He slapped his hand against the stone wall. "But she told me something before she died. Something I can't get out of my mind. She said they were heading towards *Armageddon*—towards the mountains west of here." He rubbed his gnarled chin, his dark eyes glinting in the candlelight. "Now, I thought in your heavenly wisdom, O Queen, you might know something about it."

Laz shook his head. "I don't know. You think it's got to do with the boy and girl showing up?"

"Usually, I think everything's got to do with the boy and girl." Now he was leaning against the wall, showing how tired he really was. "You used to say you could see things. Like the future. So that was all bullshit? Campfire stories?"

"It's true I used to be able to see some things. But then the *fucking world ended.* Now I only see what's in front of my nose, and sometimes not even that," he said. "Like right now."

"Fair enough," Ben said, satisfied with Laz's answer. He stood up straight again, dusted off his shoulder. "I'll see you tomorrow, then. We'll talk some more. I think you know the way out."

"Yes, the front door was locked. You'll come open it for me?"

Ben laughed. "You can go out the same way you came in," he said, pointing to the window.

"I've got to know," Laz said.

Ben had already anticipated the question. "You want to know if I was the one who killed your sister."

Laz looked away, then nodded.

Ben felt a lump in his dry throat, as he remembered the cave in the Cliffside. He felt the guilt of old wounds opening again. "The answer is no."

They set out at dawn. At first light, the girl waved up to the watch tower casually as if it was any other morning, making sure to do nothing out of the ordinary. "Let me do the talking," she had whispered to Adam and the dog. Above them, Smokey scanned the yellow and green horizon with binoculars before finally giving the order to open the gate. Then the old man looked down at these children with their full packs and offered a friendly wave. "Looks like you're both loaded for trouble there, Kid. Where you two deviants headed this fine morning?"

The boy answered out of instinct. "Well, we do not know, because we are running—"

Eve jabbed her elbow into his gut, taking all the wind out of him. The boy doubled over, trying to breathe.

She looked up and smiled at the old warrior. "What Adam means is, we're staying close to home today, just running around in circles probably, because we're, Um, on a new case of the detectives."

Smokey leaned over the rail. "Sounds interesting. What's the case?"

"The case?" She looked down at Dog, who was not being much help. "The case. It's the case of the missing dog, that's the case."

Smokey scratched his temple. "But there's Dog, right there."

She pushed both fists into her hips. "Hey, let kids *pretend*, okay?"

Once they were far from the wall, the girl slipped a chicken feather out of her pocket and placed it on her open palm, taking a deep breath and blowing it into the air. Then she turned to the boy. "Wherever the feather goes, we go. Okay?" The boy nodded and the dog barked in agreement. The three of them watched as the wind took it. The white feather whipped around as if in a funnel, then flew towards the river for a few yards before drifting slowly down to the hard ground.

"It's settled, then." She pointed towards the river. "We go *south*."

They had filled two hemp sacks until they were stuffed full of food, tools, extra clothes, a sewing kit, and a select dozen or so books from the basement of Carnegie; overnight, the boy's list had become extensive. Dog's soft blanket was lashed around the boy's waist with a leather string.

When they reached the riverbank, Eve slipped her pack off her shoulder and let it drop to the ground. Then she slipped out of her cotton pants and began to roll them into a ball.

The boy looked at her. "What are you doing?"

She lifted her arms to take off her shirt. "I'm getting ready to cross this river," she said, stuffing the shirt into her pack. "What do you think I'm doing?"

"I do not think this is a good idea. The river is dangerous."

Eve lashed down the cover to her bag, buckling it closed. "You can swim, can't you?"

"Of course I can swim. I have been swimming this river for a long time, a long time before you ever came here."

Dog howled in laughter.

She stepped into the water to her knees. "Okay then. Come on, prove it."

The boy bit his lip and looked away.

She had waded in up to her waist now. "Well, come on then," she yelled to him over the loud rush of water. "You keep saying you're the first explorer and all. What kind of explorer doesn't want to know what's on the other side of a river? Last one across is a Telemarketer. You too, Dog."

Adam felt the firm nudge of Dog's nose against the back of his leg.

The girl leaned forward and dunked her head into the river, whipping back up to push her wet hair away from her face. She stood there for a moment, feeling the current against her legs, before coming back a few steps towards shore. "It's not too deep right over here. Come on. Throw me my pack, and we'll hold our packs above our heads to keep everything dry. Dog, you're just going to have to paddle across."

The boy folded his arms. "And what do we do if there's a monster in there?"

She rubbed some of the cool water into her cheeks. "Only one way to find out."

There was a sound outside the walls of Armageddon that no one could place right away, an old sound none of them had heard in a very long time. From the watchtower, Smokey had heard the faint echo first, coming towards them from the south; by the time he'd rang the alarm everyone else in Armageddon had already picked it up in their ears too, a strange sound as out of place in this world as a train whistle or the howl of an airplane overhead. At first, the low rumble getting closer made everyone think, *Dragon.* But it was a machine sound. The sun was high and hot as Hyatt tinkered in the back of his workshop with the new crankshaft when he heard the echo of the familiar low, popping thrum.

"A motorcycle," he mumbled to himself, dropping the wrench in his hand as he ran outside. "Holy shit. A *chopper.*"

He let the doors to the makeshift barn behind him swing open, something he had never done before.

Outside the gate, a grizzled man with a white hair and beard revved the throttle one last time before killing the engine and using the heel of his boot to let the kickstand out. He looked younger than Hyatt, probably by at least a decade or even two. The stranger was all alone, and his bike had no gear attached to it, not even a knapsack or bedroll strapped to the back of the ragged seat. It was if he had just came by from the next town over for a quick visit. Only there was no other town.

Hyatt came closer, still mesmerized. "Is that an old soft tail?"

The stranger nodded as he stretched out his sunburnt arms. "Rides a little rough out here," he said. "But it gets you where you want to go. Friends, I heard the most peculiar rumor," he bellowed like a preacher. "I heard there was a boy and a girl here in your fair city, so I thought I'd swing on by, take a look."

"A rumor, huh?" Ben said. "Where'd you hear that from?"

"Oh, word gets around," the stranger said.

"Don't see how," Ben said, letting his suspicion out into the open. "Don't know if you've heard, but our internet's been down for quite a while."

"Yeah," Hyatt added. "About thirty years."

Ben motioned with his hands for everyone to get back inside the wall. There were some grumbles, but slowly they trudged back inside, even Hyatt.

The stranger waved both hands at Ben, who stood firm in front of him. "Well, ain't *you* the local hero. The good shepherd." The rider let out a sour laugh as he watched the others file in the gate behind Ben. "Maybe it was a little bird told me, then."

"I notice you don't carry any gear," Ben said. "Find many gas stations out there?"

The rider let out a low whistle. "Whoa. Here I am being friendly, and all I get are these crazy questions. What happened to hospitality? Ain't this the great state of Texas?"

"It *was*," Ben said, still sizing up this man who appeared out of the blue. "But I think you knew that. And you'll get no hospitality here. Friend."

The stranger nodded, looked around some more. "So be it. I can already see the boy and the girl ain't here anyway. So I got to be moving on." He kicked up the stand on his bike, suddenly impatient. "Hey, hero, if I do see them out there, I'll be sure to let them know you're looking for them." He kicked the bike to life and revved the throttle a few times, leaving Ben to choke in a cloud of black vapor. The bike dug into the loose dirt as he peeled out, heading due west, towards the mountains and those purple clouds that still hovered above them like a crown.

Ben waited for the rider to disappear out of sight before he turned back to the watchtower. "Smokey, where's Eve and the Kid?"

"Out there somewhere," Smokey yelled back, already searching the horizon with his binoculars. "The girl said they were looking for a missing dog that's not missing."

Ben didn't have time to argue. Whoever this biker was, he wasn't human, Ben was sure of it. He felt the slow drip of panic seeping into his bones. "Send a couple of the boys out to find them, bring them back," he called up to the tower. Then he turned back to the mountains, looking in vain for any signs of the rider as he headed west. He had already disappeared, like a ghost from his memory.

A few passing clouds brought rain, wetting the crumbled ground under their feet and turning thirsty dust into slicks of red mud. The boy and the girl made a game of who could slide the farthest without falling. Dog watched from a rock as the two humans skated on their smooth sandals in every direction, lifting his head every so often to catch some of the raindrops on his outstretched tongue. "Come on, Dog," the girl said. "Try it. Four feet are better than two."

"Dogs don't slide," he said. "We creep, and we dart. But we never slide."

"Chicken," she said, knowing full well this was probably the worst thing to call a dog who spent its life guarding chickens.

Dog pretended to ignore her. "That's fine," he said finally, licking the wet fur on his leg. "Just don't start calling me *human*."

Now the clouds had passed for the moment, revealing a yellow midday sky and leaving them in the hot bake of sun. Up ahead, they could see rounded clumps of brown dotting the top of a wide ridge. The boy squinted under his outstretched hand in the sunlight. "What is that?"

"Trees," the girl said, passing him.

Adam stood there for a moment, perfectly still, rolling the word off his tongue. *Trees. Trees. Trees.* "I have never observed a tree before," he called out as he ran to catch up with her. Until now, he had only seen them in books, as illustrations and in the background of photographs. In the pictures he'd seen, there were trees everywhere in Texas, all different shapes and sizes. He wondered if people took trees for granted if there were so many, all over the place. To him, they were a wonder he had never seen with his own eyes, as magical as a truck or a dragon. As Adam and Eve walked quickly together, the boy tried to remember everything he had learned about trees from the basement of Carnegie, a list of knowledge pouring through his head. Trees together were called a forest. Forests could either be deciduous or coniferous. There was a coniferous tree in some place called Guam that had poisonous sap. Poets would sit under the non-poisonous trees and write their poems in the shade.

Dog galloped towards the ridge ahead of the two, to scout things out. He scampered up the now-muddy ridge and disappeared into what looked like a wall of green. A few minutes behind him, Eve and Adam climbed up the ridge together until they found themselves on the edge of a deep forest of low trees, the ground beneath their feet different now—soft with loose dirt and fallen leaves. Ahead, the trees grew so thick that the shade of their canopy made the forest look dark, foreboding. But the girl knew it would be cooler inside. As she wove her way past the first few lines of thin trees, the boy remained behind, his hand running along the smooth, almost furry bark of the first tree he'd come to, his fingers reaching for the lowest branch. "It feels differently than I thought it would feel."

The girl stopped and looked back at him with a frown. "They're just trees," she said, coming back to him and pulling on his arm. "They had them all over Alabama. All dead, like these trees are. Probably all over the world, too."

But the boy wouldn't budge, his eyes fixed on the rustling leaves above. "I wonder what this tree is called?"

Eve sighed. "What do you mean, what's it called? It's a tree. You called it *tree*."

The boy shook his head. "No, in Texas there were names for all the different kinds of trees. For example, oak tree, maple tree, giving tree."

She shook her head. "Name it whatever you want, Adam." The girl started to walk away but after a few hurried steps she stopped, thinking for a moment with a change of heart. "You know what? I guess we'll have to get used to naming things around here. Might as well start with trees." She waited there patiently as the boy took out his notebook and scribbled down something hastily. He slipped the book back into his hemp sack; instead of following her into the woods, he knelt down on one knee and cupped his hand to his ear. The forest was silent except for the chirp of a few hidden birds.

Losing her patience now, she stamped her foot into the soft earth. "What are you doing *now*?"

"Listening for the Lorax," he said. "He states for the trees."

She went to pull him up. "You read too many books," she said, dusting him off a little. "Come on, it's getting dark. Let's catch up to the dog." She stepped quickly through the thick woods, turning her head every so often to make sure the boy was following. After a while, she slowed down until they were walking side-by-side again. The boy was still deep in thought.

She tapped his arm. "What did you name it? The tree, I mean."

"I named it *Curvy-Trunk-With-Thin-Branches* tree," he said, smiling with pride as he puffed his thin chest out a bit. "What do you think?"

She tried to stifle a laugh. "I think we're going to need more practice naming stuff, that's what I think."

They reached the other end of the dense woods as the sun began to set. The landscape now widened into wide open country again, with lonely scrubs of dead brush and soft plumes of brown grass dotting the rolling hills, all the way to the horizon. "More desert," the boy said, crestfallen. He was hoping that the trees were a sign of other new things to come, those natural miracles of the old world he had only studied in books: waterfalls, volcanoes, giant redwoods, whirlpools that could swallow ships, drive-in movie theatres, and of course, pickup trucks. He was certain all the explorers of Texas had felt exactly like this, so long ago:

Coronado, John Glenn, Byrd, Vasco da Gama. He would tell this to the girl, but she wouldn't be interested in history. She probably had no idea who the explorers were, anyway, he thought.

From over the hill, Dog had picked up their scent and sprinted towards them, almost totally out of breath as he approached. The fur on his legs and belly was matted down with damp dirt. "I found a cave up ahead," he panted excitedly, his tongue hanging loosely over his teeth. "It's a strange kind of cave, though."

She patted the top of his head. "Good work, Dog." He licked her hand.

"Any water around?" the boy asked. "We will need fresh water soon."

Dog nodded. "There's a small pool, behind that rise."

The boy came closer when he noticed specks of fresh blood on his friend's snout. Dog smiled back at him, licking his chops. "There's definitely plenty of fish in it." Even though he was tired, the dog hopped from front legs to back in front of them, excited by the whole new range of smells this place provided.

Adam looked around, breathing in deeply too, filling his lungs with what felt like different air. This feeling also must have been the same for the old explorers of Texas. "So this is what the other side of the world looks like," he announced loudly, his arms outstretched.

"Hold on there, Magellan. We've only been gone one day," Eve said. She took out her water bag and lifted it to her lips.

"There's probably a lot more to see. Let's check out this cave first."

They followed Dog through the rolling hills of loose, dry soil and grass. There was a shock of purple wildflowers growing out from under a rock; Eve stopped to pick some and wove them together as she walked. She found more over the next crest and added them, making a kind of twisted crown. "This is for you," she said to the boy. "For the first explorer."

"Thanks," he said, holding it at a distance in his hands. "But flowers are for girls."

"Who says *that*?"

"The rules say that," the boy said. "The world has rules. It is all written down. The rules state flowers are for girls, and football is for boys. The rules are all written in the basement of Carnegie, if you care to read them."

She stopped cold, folding her slender arms across her chest.

"Do not stare at me like that," he said, looking away. "I did not construct the rules."

"Listen," she said softly, the calm in her voice surprising him. "Look around, Adam. We *are* the rules." She stepped closer and her hand found his; they stood that way for a while, close to one another, both realizing how alone they truly were at that moment. The dog's bark reminded them it would soon be dark. The rain clouds were moving back in again, threatening another downpour. When they reached the crest of the next hill and looked down, they both stopped cold in their tracks, their mouths dropped open.

"That's where I found the cave," Dog said proudly, pointing down to the valley below. "In there."

There, half-covered by an ancient mudslide, stood the ruin of an old building, its stone and concrete ribs sticking straight out of the hardened mud like bleached bones on a carcass. The roof was long gone and only hints of the old walls remained, but from their vantage point they could see it had been a big structure, two or three stories, bigger even than the Carnegie back in Armageddon.

At first Smokey thought it was just another one of those stray birds, flying east over Armageddon; the black cormorants and crows had been escaping the mountains for weeks, buzzing his watchtower as they searched for the sea. He saw the lone black dot suspended in the bright yellow sky and figured it would buzz overhead at any moment, even buzz his tower. But after a moment, the dot did not get bigger.

He felt a lump growing in his throat. Smokey could see this was no bird.

The black dot grew to a smudge but it was still far on the horizon. Whatever it was, it was going to be a lot bigger than a seabird. More like a zeppelin, he thought. The old hero got to his feet and leaned over the railing of the watchtower, reaching for the binoculars to take a better look. If it was a Telemarketer or some other creature they heard at night, this would be a first, to see one dare the daylight.

Who knows, he laughed to himself, shaking his head.

We had a guy on a motorcycle the other day, maybe now we're getting a helicopter. Or a fucking flying saucer. It was a strange world, but at least he could wake up every day and say, it couldn't get any stranger. He rubbed his tired eyes and lifted the heavy glasses to scan the western sky, hoping to pick it up.

His mouth fell open. The binoculars clattered to the steel floor.

He fumbled for the bell rope, tripping over the stock of his gun that was propped against the railing. The rifle began to slip over the side but Smokey caught its strap as it fell to the dirt below. His breath came ragged now, suddenly finding it hard to make sounds come out of his mouth, much less words.

"Dragon!"

The boy descended the hill first, taking the steep slope in switchbacks until he jumped to the bottom. He circled the ruin, his open hand running against the smooth stone until he found what must have been the entrance. The girl stood behind him, neither really sure what to say. Engraved in white stone in what was left of the crumbled wall beside the doorway was the letters *P.S. 43* and below it, the year *1971*.

Adam lifted his arm to trace the deep grooves of the letters and numbers with his finger. "It is written in English. This was called a *prison*," he said with a tone of amazement, peering inside the ruin. "This was the place boys and girls went every day, to learn about Texas. The boys would fight in a tournament called football. The girls would watch the football, and dance and sing."

Eve stuck out her tongue. "Well, that sounds fucking horrible."

Dog came out from inside the ruin. The clouds had opened and cold rain had begun to fall around them. The dog nudged the girl's leg with his nose. "Come on, the cave is down here."

As they picked their way across the scattered rubble, the boy became even more excited as he imagined the walls and what had been on them: he guessed all sorts of maps, the periodic table of elements, perhaps a photograph of Texas heroes like Herodotus or Benjamin Franklin. He stared at the rubble and imagined rooms with straight rows of desks, doors with numbers and names on them, and larger desks in the front of each room for the teacher. He imagined himself sitting in the front row and talking with his teacher about history or mathematics or literature. Standing there, he was so deep into the daydream he caught himself raising his hand, as if to answer a question. He imagined a bell ringing, and streams of other boys and girls running down the hallway past him. He smelled the lunchroom, where he would sit with all the other boys and girls and open his own beige bag made of paper to find the food his mother and father had prepared for him that morning, in the family. He imagined the conversations he would have while he ate his food. *It is Friday, the night of the big game*, he imagined himself asking the boy next to him as they ate their food. *Are you excited for the football tonight?*

Oh yes, I am very excited to observe the football, the other boy replied. *Will you drive your pickup truck to the football?*

Adam nodded. *There will be poontang in our pickup trucks tonight*, he whispered back.

"Who are you talking to?" the girl asked.

"No one," Adam stuttered, coming back from his dream. He rubbed his eyes and coughed. "I believe Dog went in this direction." He started walking away.

They followed the dog's tracks through the ruins until they were standing directly in the center of what must have been a huge building. There was a staircase leading down into total darkness, but it was partially choked by a layer of dried mud and rocks. Now the rain started to come hard down on their heads. Somehow it had become darker quickly; there was no moon, and the twilight sky was covered with belts of high clouds. The boy and the girl stood at the mouth of the cave in silence, looking down into its blackness, their backs chilled with their own sweat and now the new rain. From below, Dog barked encouragement; the girl shrugged her shoulders and began to pick her way down the steps into the darkness.

"Wait," the boy said, pulling the candle lantern from his bag and lighting it with the flint strike.

She smiled at him. "Good work. It's about *time* you made yourself useful."

He stared blankly back at her. In his mind, he had already calculated a list of all the ways he had been very useful on this journey so far. There were seventeen items on the list already.

"Oh come on, it was just a joke," she said, laughing.

"Oh," he said, wondering if this Alabama girl knew *joke* was just another word for *lie*.

He held the lantern above his head and took the steps tentatively, one at a time. She followed right behind him, her hand on his shoulder as they descended. The mud made their footing uneven and tricky. The stone steps dipped down until they reached a set of closed double doors that looked like they were made of metal, a few old flakes of white paint still attached to them here and there. The mudslide had blocked the bottom half of the doors. As they stepped closer, they saw a sign hanging above the doorway. Dog stood at the doors, sniffing at the tight crack between them. The boy raised the lantern to read the faded sign, the girl right behind him.

"It is in English," he announced. *"Girls' Locker Room."*

Eve smiled. "Well, boys, I guess this is as far as you can go," she said. When the boy turned to her with another blank stare, she sighed. "Another joke!"

Each of the doors had a bars attached across the middle. The boy tested one with his free hand, then the other, but they didn't budge. "I believe these doors open inwards, and these bars somehow open them." They seemed rusted in place, not budging an inch with his weight against them.

"What about this," Dog said, pointing a paw towards a large, rusted box attached to the wall next to the left door, about two feet above the floor. It had air vents in every side.

"That was called a *drinking fountain*," the boy said, holding the lantern closer. "Prisons had many of them all over. People were thirsty back then. You see, water would come from the top. In Texas, the girls would stand around them and watch the boys walk by."

"You're making all this up," Eve said. "Prisons, drinking fountains, football."

"I do not make things up," the boy answered sharply. "I am just repeating what is written in books."

Together, the three of them leaned their shoulders against the double doors and pushed hard, but nothing moved.

"Maybe we're going to have to dig it out," Dog said. "Dogs are good diggers."

"Hold on a minute. Let's get a running start first," Eve said, slipping off her hemp sack and laying it behind her on the ground. Adam set the lantern down on the drinking fountain and they stepped back to the edge of the stairway. Dog stood between them, lowering his head and scratching at the hard mud with his front paw like a bull getting ready to charge. The boy and girl looked at each other. "Wait a second," the boy said. "We should spit into our hands and rub them together. In Texas, when people had to move something heavy, they always did that."

In the dim light, Eve looked down at her hands, then at the door ahead. "Why?"

"I am not exactly sure why, but it usually worked."

The girl shrugged, then spit into one hand and rubbed her palms together. Dog licked one paw and did the same thing. "Now we're ready," the boy said. He nodded and the girl nodded back, her lips pursed. Dog barked, and from a crouch they all flew at the doors, running as fast as they could. Dog reached them first, his forepaws outstretched. Then the boy and girl slammed into the doors at the same time, both of them gasping as their shoulders rang with pain. The two doors creaked open, the old rust holding them together giving way. They slumped there on the floor for a while, getting their wind back.

"Yeah, the spit definitely was the clincher," she said, rubbing her throbbing shoulder.

"You are joking again."

She nodded. "Exactly."

They both got to their feet and peered inside the crack between the doors. The air coming out of the crack was musty and dense, like a tomb. Adam thrust the lantern inside. Mud only covered the first few yards of the floor. Beyond that, there was only total darkness. "You got any more of those candles?" she asked. He nodded, handing her the lantern as he searched his bag.

Dog put his snout between the doors and took a long sniff. "Smells okay."

Adam lit another candle off the lantern and they slipped inside. Dog crept ahead of them, quickly disappearing into darkness. In the orange glow of candlelight, they could see rows of metal containers ahead of them, stacked two high.

The squared tile floor looked clear of any debris. The grey rows trailed off into the dark. "Those are the lockers," the boy whispered.

"I figured that out," Eve whispered back. She took a few steps forward. "Hello?" she said loudly, hoping no one answered back. The only reply was the echo of her own voice against the walls. Some of the locker doors were open, but some still had locks on them. The room had the feel as if it had just been left, and that people would be back to use it at any minute.

"I wonder what happened to all the kids who owned this stuff," Eve said wistfully.

Adam opened one of the empty lockers and peered inside. "They are probably all in Disneyland now."

Between the rows of lockers were thin wooden benches bolted into the floor. The boy and the girl walked deeper into the cavernous room. A piece of cloth was draped on one of the benches closest to them. Eve put down her lantern and picked the cloth up gently and stretched it out. It was some kind of shirt, red with short sleeves, made for someone about her size. "I can't read this," she said, holding it closer to the light. There was writing around a giant pair of pink lips.

"It was called a tee shirt," the boy said, coming closer. "It says, *"Girls Just Wanna Have Fun."*

She smiled, slipping her tattered Alabama shirt over her shoulders and then replacing it with this new one. "Well, I like this already." It hugged her shoulders well enough, but the boy pointed to her waist, noticing the shirt only reached halfway down her torso.

"It is too small," Adam said.

"I don't know—I think it's perfect," she said, smoothing her hand across her bare stomach. From habit, she would always tap her index finger against the spot where her belly button should be, a constant reminder to herself that she was different. They were both different in that way. She knew even the girl in the picture book The Little Mermaid had a belly button, and she was half fish. "What do *you* think, Dog?"

Dog came out of the darkness, sniffing around the base of the bench. "Just as long as it's not a sweater."

They went down the row of lockers, clicking any of the handles that would open, holding up their lanterns to the doors like archaeologists inspecting a lost tomb. "Hey," the girl said, opening the last in the row and looking inside. With her free hand she pulled out another piece of clothing, much bigger and heavier than the shirt. It was a dark red or brown with white sleeves and it had writing in English stitched across the back, in big white letters: *MOUNT TABOR FOOTBALL* around what looked like a big egg with stitches in it. The front had round white buttons and a name written across the heart in script: *Stevie G.*

When she held it up to the light, a spider dropped out of one of the sleeves. "Yeah, *sorry*," she said to it as the spider scurried away on the floor. Then Eve found a loop in the collar of the coat and let it twirl on her finger for him to see. She was smiling. "What's this?"

"That's the coat of a football player," Adam said. "I believe the correct term was, *letter jacket*."

"Oh, I can see that," she said, clearly beaming. "But what's it doing in a *girl's* locker?"

Dog sighed. "Sounds like another mystery."

The boy cleared his throat. "There is no mystery. The story is obvious: a girl who attended this prison had poontanged a boy from another prison. This boy was named Stephen. She forgot his letter jacket when she went to Disneyland. Mystery solved."

Eve thought for a moment, then shook her head. "No, I'm going with another story. You see, once upon a time there was actually a girl on the football team named Stevie," she said. "And she drove her own pick-up truck. And she won every football tournament singlehanded."

"That makes no sense," the boy said. "Besides, Stevie was a name for a boy."

The dog turned away with a yawn, ready to find a spot for sleep.

"Maybe," she said. "But I think stories are better when they make no sense. That way, they can surprise you." She twirled the coat one last time on her finger before tossing it to the boy. "Here you go, Stevie," she said. "It's a little too big for me."

He furrowed his brow. "But we are the same size."

"It's a metaphor," she said. "Poets use them a lot."

He held it in his hands for a moment, feeling the material and holding it like it was some kind of golden fleece, thinking about its history and who wore it in the old world. When he put it on over his shirt, the girl looked him over with an approving look. For that second, he looked like a completely different boy, and she was trying to figure out why. "It suits you," she said.

"Do you really think so?"

She tilted her head a bit, then nodded in the dim light. "It looks like you earned it." Before she closed the locker, she noticed something etched into the back of the dim metal box. "Hey, bring that lantern closer."

Adam stepped towards her and held up the light. Scrawled into the red paint inside the locker was a strange symbol:

"Stevie plus Geraldine," she read. "It's inside a heart."

"I think that was the symbol to show two people were in love."

She traced her finger along the curved edges of the heart, saying the same words with wonder under her breath a few times: *Stevie loves Geraldine. Stevie loves Geraldine. Stevie loves Geraldine.*

"There is more," the boy said, pulling her away.

At the other end of the room, an open door led to a smaller chamber. A sign screwed into the metal door read *TRAINING ROOM*. Inside the cramped chamber, two raised tables covered with blue cushions ran parallel to each other. There were empty shelves on either side, a few empty containers strewn about.

The girl looked around the cramped room and started yawning, suddenly worn down after a day filled with so much walking. "This seems like a good place to make camp for the night. How much of the hemp seed do we have left? I'm starving." The boy tossed her the bag of food and she put a handful in her mouth, chewing quickly. She washed each swallow down with a swig of her water jug. "You two hungry?" she said, holding out the bag, her mouth half-full.

Dog shook his head, then hopped up on the left table and circled a few times, testing the cushion with the weight of his paw. "This one's mine," he said, dropping down in the middle. "For dogs only." His eyes shut almost immediately. He began to snore loudly.

The boy and the girl looked at one another.

"I guess this one's for the humans," Adam said, slipping off his pack. He found a bare spot on the shelf above their bed for the lantern. Its candle would run out soon. He rolled his new jacket off his shoulders and let it slump to the floor. His shirt was drenched with the day's sweat and rain, so he slipped it over his head and draped it on the back of a metal chair to dry.

From the door, the girl watched him as he moved in the flickering shadow. She decided she liked the way his hands always hugged his thin waist when he was preparing to do something. In the dim candle light, she decided he was handsome. She wondered if they would still be friends if there were hundreds of other kids their age around this prison, instead of only two. Eve kept watching as he hoisted himself up onto the tall cushioned table and slid over until his right arm was pressed against the concrete wall, leaving her most of the space on the bed.

She smiled at that. He reached over for his bag and propped it behind his head as a makeshift pillow. "Good night," the boy called out, his voice already heavy with sleep. "Do not let the insects bite you."

Eve finished eating and hopped up beside him, blowing out one of their candles before taking off her own soaked shirt and laying it on the same chair to dry. In the darkness, she slid down against the boy and lay completely still, her arms rigid. They had never slept together before in the same room, and now it felt completely strange laying here, feeling the boy's steady breathing against her own for the very first time, his heart slow, ready for sleep. But she was wide awake, suddenly remembering all the stories Cookie would tell her before it was time for sleep; the stories about men. Men and boys. Eve pressed her fingers into the boy's arm to see if he was still awake. When the boy didn't move, she pushed again, harder this time.

"*I cannot find the keys to my pick-up truck*," the boy shouted, waking from a dream. He rubbed his face.

"What? No, listen," the girl said. "Cookie told me everything I need to know about, well, you know," she said, her hands moving up and down like fluttering birds. "About what a boy wants from a girl."

The boy moaned, still half-asleep. "What does a boy want from a girl?"

She sat up faced him, even though she could barely make out his face in the orange glow of the lone candle. "Like you don't know."

"To be honest, Evangeline. I do not know."

There was a long silence. "You really don't know?"

Dog barked from the other table. "Trust me. He doesn't know."

She lay back down. "Well, good. Just don't *try* anything, that's what I'm saying."

Now the boy was sitting up. "What am I supposed to try?"

"Hanky-panky, that's what. Okay? That's exactly what Cookie told me: make sure there's no *hanky-panky*." She was not sure herself what this word meant exactly, since every time Cookie had mentioned it, the old woman was mostly smoking her weeds.

They both lay still for a moment, his shoulder locked perfectly into the dip of her side. Then she felt him moving beside her, slowly turning his body away. She heard him reach for his sack and fumble it open; she listened as he took something out. There was a long silence; then she felt his elbow moving back and forth slightly against her skin in a kind of quick rhythm. She heard him mumbling something under his breath while his arm moved.

She sprang up again, pushing his arm away. "What are you doing?"

Adam lifted up his notebook in the dim candlelight. "I am writing down *hanky-panky* in my list of words I do not understand."

"Oh." She fell back and turned away, yanking the dog's blanket over her body like a cocoon, leaving the boy's body bare. The sharp whip of the blanket blew out the candle above them, leaving them in complete darkness. "Good night," she muttered, pulling her legs up to her body.

"Told you," the dog said from across the room.

Hyatt tore open the doors of his workshop with a weary grunt, letting rays of sunlight stab the darkness inside. He stomped towards the far end of the long rattletrap barn on his spindly legs, cursing under his breath. Ben and Laz followed behind him, taking in the rare sights they had been given by actually getting to look inside the building for the first time.

A few minutes before, Hyatt had been sitting with Lazlo on the steps of Carnegie, watching as Ben tried to organize search parties to fan out and find the boy and girl. They had been gone for two full days now, with no sign of them anywhere. From what they had taken along, Hyatt thought, it was pretty clear they had run away: water sacks, food, flints, candles, and the damned dog.

And then there was the dragon fly-by two days ago.

There was a lot of grumbling coming from the old heroes. Most of the men were balking at the idea of going outside the wall for what might be days or weeks, especially if they were starting at night. Even Smokey was trying to find excuses. "Chances of us finding two kids out there are about zero," Hyatt heard one of the old heroes complain.

"Yeah, Ben," another man shouted. "And now there's a fucking *dragon* out there, man."

Smokey nodded. "We're not cowards. But be reasonable, is all we're saying. Big fucking world out there."

Hyatt knew if no one volunteered to join him, Ben would go it alone. Under his wheezing breath, Hyatt cursed Smokey and the rest of those fake heroes because they *were* being cowards, right when Ben needed them the most. He cursed his own frail body, too, for being unable to do much to help, either. But there were other ways he could help his friend.

Hyatt watched the men argue until he felt he'd had enough. "Hey, Ben," he had called from the steps, jerking his head in the direction of the workshop. "Come meet a new friend of mine."

They walked back to Hyatt's workshop. Inside the doors, the old man slid a dusty, tattered canvas off a mound sitting in the corner. Ben always thought it had been a pile of old parts, junk left over waiting to find a purpose. It took Ben a while for his eyes to adjust to the light, but after a moment he realized exactly what he was looking at: a Ford pick-up truck, body style probably about 1980, give or take a decade or two.

"Surprise," Hyatt said, his withered chest puffed out. "Makes a search party much more interesting, don't you think?"

"You've been holding out on me, you old goat," Ben said, walking around the side of it.

Clearly, this was no longer any ordinary truck. There was an old snowplow welded to the front as a battering ram, painted with giant menacing snake-eyes, gnashing white teeth and a forked red tongue. Ben continued his tour around, carefully taking in every detail; the metal plates covering the wheel wells were painted with green, webbed claws. The windows had been replaced by thick steel grates that from a distance looked just like grey scales. And the tailgate had metal spikes sticking out of it. "Hey, I figured if the bad guys got a dragon out there, then we should have one, too."

"I thought you said you *were* one of the bad guys," Ben said, running his hand along the side of the truck bed.

"I changed sides," Hyatt said with a shrug. "Typical bad guy behavior. It was gonna be a present for the boy. For his birthday, bar mitzvah, whatever we call it now."

"Aw, I always knew you were a softie," Ben said.

"Whatever, big daddy. When are we leaving?"

"What? You're not going out there. You're too old to do any good."

"Fuck you, dipshit," Hyatt roared. "News flash, hero: we're *all* too old. And I'm driving. Or this truck goes bye-bye from a big block of semtex under the hood. *Boom.* Okay, amigo?"

Ben nodded. "All right. You and me. We got much BP left?"

"About twenty gallons, tops. But I rigged it so she'll run on just about anything that burns hot. I put a bottle of that corn poison in her belly yesterday, and goddamn if she don't shake like a belly dancer with the runs. Good to go. Got a few adjustments to make before we go out hunting."

Ben rolled his eyes. "We'll leave at first light. So that means you've got a few hours to get this shitbox ready." He looked around the barn. "You got any more of those bombs laying around this mad scientist's laboratory?"

The boy had read about solar eclipses before. The three of them sat on the hill overlooking the ruins, shielding their eyes as they watched the pale moon darken and edge higher towards the sun. "When this was Texas, the eclipse would occur every few years," the boy announced. "Usually they were a sign of something bad coming. This was called an *omen*." As they watched the midday sun slowly turn black on the horizon, covered by the moon, Adam told them a story he remembered from *People and Nations*: Herodotus had written of a total eclipse just as Xerxes of Persia invaded Greece, leaving the armies of the Persian king frightened in darkness as they crossed the sea. "It was a bad omen for the coming battle, because the Persians lost."

Finally, the moon covered the sun, leaving the world in a strange shadow. "This one seems like a bad omen, too."

Dog whined. "Were there any dogs in this battle? Maybe a wolf?"

"I do believe there were elephants, perhaps some lions."

"*Elephants,*" Dog muttered. "Overrated."

"Oh, yeah?" Eve looked down at him, shielding her eyes now that the sun had begun to crawl out from behind the moon again. "And how would you fight an elephant if we came across one out here? Or a lion? I'm just curious."

"You mean, how would *we* fight an elephant. We're a pack, remember. And a pack always fights together. A pack does everything together."

"Oh right, I forgot. And you're counting on *him* to fight?" They both turned to look at the boy, who had taken out his notebook and was perched on a rock, totally enveloped in his sketch the trajectory of the sun and moon above. He squinted in the new sunlight, thinking hard. After a while he looked up at them with a perplexed look on his face. "What?"

"Oh, nothing. We were just wondering if you could kill an elephant."

He shook his head. "Dog already knows, I do not think I could kill anything."

Suddenly, the world was doused in shadow again. The girl rested her hands on her hips and looked over at the boy, jerking her thumb up at the sky. "Hey genius, how many of these eclipses can you have in one day?" She was already bored with the idea of an eclipse.

He only shrugged his shoulders, intent on finishing his drawing before they moved on.

The dog was the first to look up. "It's not an eclipse," Dog said, his mouth left open as he gazed at the sun. "I think we're in trouble." He backed up a few steps, his body tensed.

The boy and the girl lifted their heads and realized this wasn't another eclipse at all: something else was blotting out the sun, something moving. Whatever it was, it was enormous. At first, the girl took it for another passing storm cloud, and cursed the constant rain they'd seen so far. But it was no cloud. It moved back and forth in the sky; the dark shadow reminded Adam of a fish in the way it moved, undulating slowly back and forth as it hovered closer and closer in the horizon. Slowly he realized the shape of it was familiar, something he'd stared at time and time again in his books.

Suddenly the boy's body went rigid. He dropped the pencil in his hand. Dog growled.

Now the girl was frozen, too. "What is it?"

The boy found it almost impossible to speak. "I believe," he whispered finally, swallowing hard. "We are observing a dragon."

A horrible roar erupted from the sky.

"I'll take your word for it," the girl muttered back, staring at the sky, then reaching for his arm and pulling him off his rock. "Let's get the fuck out of here." The boy stood up, slowly as if he was in some kind of trance, dropping his notebook from his lap as they scrambled backwards together. His heel caught on the edge of the rock and he teetered for a moment before falling headlong down the hill, tumbling more than halfway down the steep slope. The girl held onto his arm, refusing to let go, and they fell together. She yelped in pain when her knee slammed hard against a jagged rock that stuck out of the mud.

The boy was still in a state of shock; he wasn't frightened, he couldn't decide if he was inside a dream or if this was real. As it swooped closer, the dragon looked almost exactly the same as the pictures he'd studied for so long in Carnegie: the same spiked tail, the same wings, even the same colors. It was strange, as if this thing had leaped right out of his imagination, instead of the mountain above Armageddon. If he had drawn a dragon from memory yesterday, it would look precisely like this dragon.

The dragon peeled off and swung closer to the ruined school below, as if it could not see them yet. "Head back to the trees," Dog barked to them. "Run. *Run!*"

"My notebook," Adam gasped, scrambling back up the hill. He had left it where he fell.

"*Forget* the notebook," Eve said, catching his arm as she passed him.

They climbed the ridge and made it to the edge of the forest. The girl's knee throbbed with pain, streams of blood running down her leg. She felt like she couldn't walk much farther, much less run. The boy slipped her arm over his shoulder and together they limped into the canopy of the thick woods.

"Don't stop," Dog barked as he stood on the edge of the cliff they had just climbed, facing them. "I'm right behind you." The dog tried to catch his breath. He was about to turn back around to look for the dragon when he felt a hot wind brush against the fur of his back. He slowly turned around. He realized he was staring straight into the eyes of the dragon as it hovered in the air in front of him.

Dog scowled. He dug into the loose dirt with his paw, like a bull elephant. "You picked the wrong pack," he barked as loud as he could. He hoped the boy and the girl had run. His own legs felt frozen, so he probably could not run, even if he wanted to.

In the dead forest, Adam draped Eve's arm over his shoulder and helped her limp between the trees. Suddenly they both heard a horrible sound, like a sharp crack of thunder and as they ran they could sense a searing heat on the back of their necks. "Don't stop," he said to her. But she fell from exhaustion, losing too much blood. He thought of Dog and turned back to see an orange wall of fire engulfing the trees at the edge of the woods, exactly where the dog had left them. Without thinking, he ran towards the flames. "Dog!"

The girl slumped to her side, her whole leg throbbing with pain, and watched as Adam disappeared back into the maze of trees, towards black smoke. These trees wouldn't hide them for long, not against that. She gripped her leg, pressing her palm down against the gash in her knee to try and stop the bleeding. Smoke made its way past her, making her cough. A few moments later, she felt the boy's hand on her shoulder. His grip was cold, almost formal. No emotion. Adam reached for her hand and tried to help her up. She felt a burst of pain as she stumbled to her feet. "Come on," he said. "We need to move."

"What about Dog?" She noticed Adam's cheeks were hot with tears. "Should we go back for him?"

His raw eyes only glared back. "Dog is dead."

He stood at the mouth of the cave, his bare toes curled against the narrow mountain ledge. Below him was the desert, stretching out in every direction. The river was only a dark sliver in the distance, twisting into the eastern horizon. From here, the town of Armageddon appeared as barely a speck of black under the yellow sky. He closed his eyes and let the swirling winds slice against his naked body, whipping his mottled grey hair about his head. From this ledge, near the top of Mount Megiddo, he could see everything. Above him, the clouds were starting to slowly break apart, finally revealing what lay behind these barren mountains. On the other side, everything was new: thick, green forests drenched with rain. Beyond the trees there were endless green meadows shrouded in mist.

Maybe that bastard Sam was right after all, he thought: *the last shall be first, and the first shall be last.* Yes, he would be the first. He would be the one to find this girl and this boy and whisper all the secrets of the new world in their ear, before anyone else.

Once again, he would become the Serpent that hunts in the night.

He had already spoken to the girl. She would listen. The girl would be the key. Turn one, he thought, and you turn both. The boy will always listen to her.

From this mountain top, he would fly again. He would be the one to show them paradise, or else they would die. It was that simple. From here, he could feel the new world beginning, under his feet. From here, he gazed out on what was left of the old world. He was ready for things to start again, tired of lingering so long over all these graves. From here, he could see what was left of Texas: one half swallowed by the sea, the other buried under a desert.

V.
Let Birds Fly Above the Earth

Sometimes when I talk to God I get too excited and I end up asking really stupid questions. They don't start out stupid and yeah/yeah/yeah I know I should write them down but lists are ~~stupid~~ boring and when the time comes and God is sitting RIGHT THERE I get so excited my fingers shake and then I can't read my writing anyway—so I end up asking the first thing that swims through my head. (Swims!) Um, God: why can't fish swim backwards? Did you really expect a platypus to end up looking like that? In Texas, were donkeys jealous of the zebras? Did you make a giraffe's neck that long so birds wouldn't be lonely? And while we're on animals, Lord, answer me this: if you lock a dragon and an ~~angry whale~~ angel in a room, who's coming out alive? I usually get through twenty or thirty of those before God stops me and lets out a big sigh. (She sighs a lot.) She says:

Whoa, hold your horses, girl. Slow down. Why all the heavy questions? How about something light?

Well, okay God I say. Something light.
Um. What's your favorite color?

Not that light.

Um. Okay. Is it true there's no such thing as a stupid question?

Who in the world told you that?
Hyatt.
That figures. No, that's actually ~~horse shit~~ wrong. In fact, most questions are pretty stupid.
All right, next question.

Um. Lord, what does *hold your horses* mean?

It was a nice way of saying STOP. It was a metaphor. Poets used a lot of those. Sometimes they used them too much, if you know what I mean. I remember one poet named Wordsworth, and he—whew! Every other line, this guy!

(God laughs—it's like a thundercloud)

Hey, you know something? This is actually kind of fun.

What else you got, girl?

For once I am out of questions. But I don't want Her to leave/
so I show God my shirt and I say, did you come up with *Girls Just Wanna Have Fun?*
No, Cyndi Lauper wrote that.
Was she a poet, too?
Oh, yes. One of the very best.
Um. So in Texas, could all women be poets? When God doesn't answer right away I get nervous because this may have been the question that killed a camel ... Finally She says:

Wow. Can I steal that?

Steal what? (I don't own anything but my notebook, and sorry, no one's getting that.)

What you just said: *could all women be poets.* That's pretty smart.

I put my hand over my mouth because that's what you did in Texas when you didn't want someone to see when you were laughing. And this is God, so/
I say: of course you can steal it. I mean, you're my Sweet Lord.
Then, it's true?

Now that I think about it—definitely.

Even Cookie?

Well, maybe almost all women.

And sometimes when I get too excited, God asks me the questions to calm me down and I like that so much because She really listens to what I say!

Child tell me again why you think paragraphs are stupid?

(Paragraphs were these little square rooms everyone in Texas had to write their books in.) And I ~~always~~ tell her the truth. I say Lord, sometimes a girl just don't feel like going all the way across the page.

Oh child, I know what you mean. And do you feel the same about sentences?

Yup. Stupid.

Quotation marks? Semi-colons?

Stupid and double stupid. No offense God but it all just seems like more ways to put things into categories: grammar, punctuations, the whole kitten/canoodle. That's why I like poetry: you don't have to worry about rules all the time. You kind of make them up as you go, right God? She smiles.

That's my girl. Do you want to know a secret?

I say, does a bear wear a funny hat?
Now where in the world did you learn *that*?
Hyatt.
I guess I already knew that. Anyway.
~~While you're in a good mood~~, Lord, can I ask you another
light question?

Girl, do you want to know a secret or not?
Sorry God.
It's okay. Did you know that in the beginning, everything
was poetry?

I say, I did *not* know that. Wow! Can I steal that?

Of course. What's Mine is yours. Someday you'll realize
all writing is stealing.
I don't really understand that one, God—but can I steal
it too, just in case? (She smiles.)
That's my girl.

Any advice before you go God?
Yes. Keep writing poems.
And by the by, child: fish can totally swim backwards
And never, ever bet against an ~~angry whale~~ angel

In the beginning, everything was poetry.

Before God invented water or air or amoebas or even sunlight, there was poetry. Poetry was older than day or night. But then God got really lonely and decided to fill up Texas with people and caterpillars and koala bears so She could hear them all laugh and sing. The ones God created first were the poets, because they had to come up with the songs. The poets were the ones who made up names for everything: teeth, elbows, despair, geometry, Venus, venus fly-traps, Alabama, every little thing. If they thought long enough, poets could find all the answers. In the beginning, when you wanted to know what love was or what lived on the bottom of the sea, you asked a poet. If you wanted to know how to build a wooden chest, sure/sure/sure you asked a carpenter, but when you wanted to know what to put in the chest or what words to carve in the lid or what it meant to the people you gave it to when you died, a poet told you. In the beginning, it was the poets who knew just about everything. They were special!

What I'm trying to say is: the poets were the ones who knew how to talk to God.

But then someone really ~~stepped in feces~~ made a mistake/because people started giving poetry *rules.* I'm not sure when it happened exactly, but there's a dusty book inside Carnegie by a man named Aristotle who tried to put poetry into ~~cages~~ categories. Categories! For poetry! I think he had four of them: comedy, tragedy, music and ~~another one I can't remember~~ epic poetry. Come on, Mister Aristotle: how can you fit the oldest, biggest, most AMAZING thing in the entire world into four tiny boxes?

Sweet Lord!

I wish I had Old Aristotle here right now, I'd sure give him a big chunk of my brain.

a ~~Play~~ Poem!
written by
~~me~~ Evangeline!

(*The curtain rises. There are two chairs facing each other in the middle of the stage. Evangeline comes out first and sits down in the left chair. She looks very ~~serious~~ prepared. Then an old man with a beard and wearing a baggy white blanket and sandals comes out. When the audience sees this man, they mumble a lot of ~~donkey shit~~ not-nice things under their breath.*)

Evangeline:(*Stands to greet old man*) Thanks for meeting me here on such short notice, sir.

Aristotle: (*Sits down*) I am always happy to educate the young people. How can I help you,

my child? Would you like to hear my latest theory on …

Evangeline:Whoa/whoa/whoa, hold your horses there, Aristotle. I'll do the educating today.

Aristotle:(*Looks around, like he doesn't understand.*) I do not understand.

Evangeline: Hold your horses? Oh, it's a metaphor. It means STOP.

Aristotle:No, I meant to say, I don't understand why I'm here, talking to you.

Evangeline:(*Turns to audience and rolls her eyes*) You're telling me. (*Audience laughs a lot*) Today, Aristotle, we're talking about poetry. And I think we need to clear a few things up, don't you?

Aristotle:Well, I am not going to sit here and let some little girl lecture me on poetry.

Evangeline:Um. Why not?

Aristotle:(*Throws up hands*) Because I am Aristotle! I wrote the book on poetry! It's called

Poetics! Look it up! There wouldn't be any poetry if it wasn't for me!

Evangeline:Um. Sorry but I happen to know the very first poet was a woman. Her name was SAPPHO. Ring any bells?

Aristotle:(*Coughs violently, ruffles his blanket*) How in Disneyland did you learn that?

Evangeline:I read books, too, Aristotle. Now in this book of yours—which by the way is super short!—you say poetry has to fit into one of four cages categories. Categories? For poetry? (*Audience cups hands around mouths and says: booooooo*) How do you explain that, sir?

Aristotle:I believe I wrote *five* categories. Everyone always forgets the dithyrambs.

Evangeline:Um. Please don't dodge the question, sir.

Aristotle:(*Smiles an old-person smile to be charming*) You know, when you talk like that, you sound just like Sappho.

Evangeline:Exactly. Now—don't you agree that in the beginning, everything was poetry?

Aristotle:Preposterous! If *everything* is poetry, then do you include, say, animal noises?

Evangeline:You ever heard a bird sing? A bee hum in your ear? Trust me, it's poetry.

Aristotle:And what about …

Evangeline:It's poetry!

Aristotle: But you didn't let me say anything.

Evangeline: Look, it doesn't matter. I already know the answer's going to be poetry.

Aristotle:All right. (*Thinks hard.*)What if I said, God?

Evangeline:Whoa! Check out the big brain on Aristotle. That's a sneaky one. But the answer is still poetry.

Aristotle:(*Folds his arms*) So God is poetry?

Evangeline:That's right. God is one big beautiful poem.

Aristotle:(*Laughs. Does not cover mouth, which is rude*) And just how do you know?

Evangeline: Oh, trust me Aristotle I know! God is definitely a poem

because a poem can do absolutely anything

(*Right then, at least ~~thirty~~ a hundred girls about the same size as Evangeline suddenly come out on the stage and start dancing to the poem "Girls Just Wanna Have Fun" by Cyndi*

Lauper. Each girl dances the way she wants. ~~There are no boys dancing~~. Okay there are ~~three~~ two boys ~~and one looks kind of like Adam~~, but they are not having as much fun because ~~Cyndi Lauper did not write this poem for them~~ they are not girls.)

I wish I knew more about Sappho. All I know is she was the first poet in her world/just like I'm the first poet in mine

And I know she wrote: a poem should treat words like butterflies

  Oh Sappho oh yes/yes/yes! Let them   *breathe*
give them lots of room to explore!

so when butterflies accidentally bump into other butterflies they won't be so   shy:

they'll smile and look the other butterfly right in the eye and say *excuse me!*

instead of just looking down at their feet/and who knows maybe they'll even start a conversation

Sometimes God is just not in a good mood. When that happens/I try to keep the stupid questions to a minimum, because I don't want to be a nuisance. Plus, when She's not feeling so good—well, God can be pretty scary. I know there's a lot in Her bowl right now/with one world ending and a whole new one about to begin. Not to mention there's a DRAGON on the loose like it's running out of fashion.

I guess it's like Cookie always says: they're not long, these days of guns & roses! even when you're God.

I am sitting on my rock when I hear God sigh (it sounds just like a big wave punching a beach)

Child, have you ever wanted to start over?

Um. Yeah! Every day! Try writing a poem God!

I believe I've written a few.

Sorry God. I forgot you kind of invented the whole thing.

That's okay, my girl.

Can I complain a little Lord?

You can even complain a lot. Talk to me, child.

Um. Writing poems is frustrating! One day I write a poem I think is really good, I mean *really* good, like cats wearing pajamas, and the next day I wake up and I look at it again and I kind of want to throw up!

I know what you mean.

Can I ask you a question about Disneyland? It's pretty light.

Why not.

Cookie told me there's an old man with a clipboard at the gate when you get there. Is that true?

What do you think, child?

Um. I think Cookie made up a big story, that's what I think.

Yes, It does sound a bit silly. Most stories are, I'm afraid.

You don't really enjoy writing stories, do you?

That is very true, God. They're so depressing!

Really? Why?

Think about it, Sweet Lord: sooner or later stories all have to end. I *hate* that.

Who in the world told you that?

Aristotle. In his book, anyway.

~~Fucking Athens.~~ That figures! Well that's another piece of ~~donkey shit~~ untruth. Did you know most stories live longer than the people in them? It's true. And as long as people want to tell it, a story can keep going forever in a circle, round and round, so it never really ends. Do you understand?

Um. Sort of, Lord. If it's like a circle, then that means a story can end at the beginning, right? So, Adam and me are the end of the story, but we're also the beginning?

Wow. You really are smart as a whip, you know that?

Thanks Lord! Wait. That's a metaphor, too, isn't it?

Right again, child. Now, have you ever tried writing your own stories, like Adam?

~~Does a bear wear~~ Um! Believe me, I have! Let me go back in my notebook here. Okay! Listen to this:

~~Once upon a time there was a girl named Eve/She woke up one morning feeling like she wanted to run away/Then she told Adam about it/Then they decided to run away together/Then they told their friend Dog about it and he decided to come too/Then they all got ready for their journey/And then on the day they decided to run away/they left early~~

Um. See! That sure didn't go well. Sorry God!

A real page-turner, girl!

See what I mean? That's the big problem with stories.

Sweet Lord. You always have to worry about what happens next. Who *cares* about what comes next? blah/blah/blah I want to know what the rocks smell like after it rains, and what the mud feels like in between your toes while you go from place to place. You know God: the important stuff!

That's my poet.

Um! ~~You sound like you're in a good mood now~~ so Can I ask you one more light question?

Why not! We're on a roll!

(Another metaphor!) Is there a reason Adam and me don't have belly buttons like old people?

There is.

Um. But you're not going to tell me, right?

I'm not. At least not right now. But—do you like your body? I mean, are you comfortable in your own skin?

I look down at my skin and I say: you know what, it *is* pretty comfortable. Thanks for asking, God.

Good. But it's not always going to feel like that.

It's not?

No it's not. (She lets out a sigh SO BIG the gust of wind kind of knocks me over) There's some big challenges ahead, for you both. There'll be reasons for that, too.

Um. Is it true that there's a reason for everything?

Well *that* is true.

Is that why Dog had to die?

Um. Now *that* is one heavy question.

Sorry God. I guess I got excited again. Poets get curious, and we can't stop.

It's okay. Do you miss him?

I sure do. I know Adam misses him even more. Can I ask if Dog made it to Disneyland? Is there a Disneyland just for dogs, or will we see him again?

What do you think?

Oh yes/yes/yes! I know he is running around in green meadows with other dogs and playing dog-jokes on everyone when they aren't looking! Then at night he sits by a fire on the warm blanket I made for him and he just howls/howls/howls to his heart's contempt. And if Cookie is right and there IS an ~~old man named Pete~~ old dog named Pete with a clipboard at the door who stops Dog and asks him, *what good things have you done in your life?* I know Dog will speak right up and say: Listen here, Pete, I saved Adam and Eve from a fire-breathing serpent! (A real dragon!) Also, I saved a mule, and I let the mule take all the credit!

Careful, girl! You just told a pretty good story there!

I did? Sorry God. Sorry!

And then BOOM God laughs like a ~~windstorm tornado tsunami crazy moose~~ hurricane

(hey—Metaphor!)

Um. So God I guess asking questions about the DRAG-ON is out of the question?

God?

Um. Are you there?

That's my girl.

Now I know why the world ended.

It ran out of poetry! It wasn't because of water, or air, or even sunshine. Poets are the real explorers, and at the end of the world, there was nothing left to explore. There was nothing new! Everybody knows you can only write so many times on one piece of paper, before it starts to fall apart. So that's what happened to Texas, I know it. At the end of the world, just about everything had been put into more ~~cages~~ categories: even people. In the beginning, poets could do anything. They could move people! They could move mountains! But in the end, the only place you learned about poets was when you went to Prison. In the end, Poetry was something you *had* to take, like medicine or bad advice. How could you forget about poetry? How could you forget about the first poet?

~~Another Play~~ Poem!
by
Evangeline

(*The curtain rises. Evangeline and Sappho are sitting on*

the stage, facing each other. They look like they have been talking for hours.)

Evangeline: I'm so excited to finally talk to you Sappho! I had no idea what you looked like

because there's no pictures of you anywhere. But you are so stately and beautiful, like a Queen! And I love your purple hair!

Sappho:Oh, thanks, honey. Truth is, you wouldn't know anything about me *at all* if old

Aristotle and Alcaeus and the rest of the boys had their way, back then.

Evangeline:Tell me about it! We had Aristotle on stage earlier in this notebook, and whew! He was not very nice.

Sappho: Honey, I could tell you stories about Aristotle that would make your boobs fall

off. (*Whispers.*) Two words: *premature ejaculation.* That's a tale for another time, but I've got to tell you, a girl couldn't touch the hem of his toga without that thing going off, you know?

Evangeline:Um. I don't know what any of that means (*She is lying here, but only a little, because Cookie says boobs a lot.)*

Sappho:Right! Well, you are a little young. You will, though. Let me ask you something: you got a sweetheart?

Evangeline:(*Face becomes redder.*) Okay first question for you, Sappho. When did you know you were a poet?

Sappho:Um. I knew I was a poet/because I wanted to

know the answer to EVERYTHING.

Evangeline:Exactly! And you say "Um" just like me! I love you so much, Sappho.

Sappho:I love you, too, honey. (*Pauses a long time.*) So, do you love Adam?

Evangeline:What kind of question is that?

Sappho: Um! So you *do* love him. (*Begins writing in her own notebook.*)

Evangeline:Wait/wait/wait! What are you writing there?

Sappho:What do you think I'm writing? A poem, silly. It's a love poem, if you really want to know.

Evangeline:Well, just hold your horses there, Sappho.

Sappho:Too late, Eve. Want me to read it out loud?

Evangeline:NO/NO/NO/NO/NO/NO.

Sappho:Sounds like I touched a nerve there. You okay?

Evangeline:Of course. Um. Second question. What's Disneyland like?

Sappho:What's Disneyland?

Evangeline:It's the place you go when you die.

Sappho. Right! We called it something else back then.

Evangeline:So you've been there? Great! Is there a man ~~or a dog or anyone with a clipboard~~ asking you questions at the gate?

Sappho:Yup. When I got there, I thought they were going to ask if I've been a good little girl all my life. So I'm ready with this long list of all this ~~donkey shit~~ stuff I made up, like *#32 I helped an old lady chase a dog off her lawn,* but I hate lists, so –

Evangeline:Hey I hate lists, too!

Sappho: Right! But they didn't ask me about that. They asked: did you dance in the river

when you had the chance, or did you just stand there like a dummy and let the fish have all the fun?

Evangeline:I knew it! I knew it! What did you say, what did you say?

Sappho: What do you think I said? I looked that guy right in the eye and said: Honey,

you ever meet a poet who *didn't* know how to dance?

Evangeline:His name was Pete, right?

Sappho:No, um, I think his name was Charon. Or maybe Fred? I can't remember.

Evangeline:And was Sam waiting for you inside?

Sappho:Who is Sam?

Evangeline:You know, the son of God. Sam Davidson! The King of Disneyland!

Sappho:Honestly, never heard that name before. But that doesn't mean a thing, because

one thing I learned in the last three thousand years is, names *always* change, even

if the song remains the same. God is still God no matter what you call Her, you

know? You want my advice? Don't get too hung up on all the different names, honey. Heck, the name of the whole world has even changed about a gazillion times, depending on who you talk to. We used to call her GAIA. What's it called now?

Evangeline:They called it Texas.

Sappho:*Yeeeeesh.* Doesn't really roll off the tongue, does it? But I guess it's still better than what the ol' Egyptians came up with: *Geb.* Ouch! Sounds like a baby trying to eat mashed prunes: *geb geb geb.* Don't know who came up with that one, but she wasn't a poet, I can tell you that much. Amateurs! Am I right?

Evangeline:But I thought poets are in charge of naming everything?

Sappho:We are! Or at least, we used to be. By the end of the world, a poet couldn't even

get arrested. They needed jobs! It was a dark time. Speaking of dark times—I

hear you have a DRAGON.

Evangeline:Oh, Sappho. You have no idea.

Sappho:Honeychild but I do I do! Back in the day, we had 'em all over the place, like cockroaches. Seemed like every other damn cave had a dragon living in it. We sure wrote enough poems about them, that's for sure!

Near the end of the world, some people in Texas liked to say *God is love*, but that's ~~donkey shit~~ wrong because anyone can look outside and see there's a whole lot more to this world than just *love*. If God was made out of love, what's She going to do when bad people do bad things? Send them flowers and a nice note, asking them to stop?

It must have been a really crazy world:

When Cookie was a girl, her favorite poet was a man named John Lennon

But she says as soon as he wrote   ALL YOU NEED IS LOVE!

someone shot him

Last night God woke me from my sleep. She's never done that before, and I thought it was just another hempseed dream but/

AWAKE MY CHILD I HAVE A TASK FOR THEE

This is not the God I know.

Um. You don't sound like yourself tonight, God. Are you okay? Are you angry at me?

Did I use your name in vain?

THOU SHALT ASK NO MORE QUESTIONS OF ME.

Okay now you're freaking me out Lord

You sound so much older/with all those THEES and THOUS

You echo like you're in a big seashell/Like you're angry/ or maybe the Villain in one of those old Shakespeares

SILENCE CHILD

A NEW WORLD is about TO BEGIN

AND I shall show thee PARADISE

Then God cries like a monsoon/her voice changes again/ back to the old God I like

I feel Her soft hand on my shoulder

you will LIVE in paradise

but child—

oh my sweet girl.

there's going to be a Catch.

~~Lord I know you said no more questions but~~ what's a catch?

A consequence.

A drawback.

A flaw in the system.

Um. I think I understand, Sweet Lord. Paradise is another word for a perfect place, but even Paradise is still going to have a flaw.

There's always going to be a catch, isn't there, God?

You are my smart, sweet child.

See? When you talk like that Lord/I don't feel so scared anymore

I take a big breath and I tell Her:

You are my God/just tell me what I have to do

That's my girl.

The boy really cares for you, doesn't he?

Not what I expected. But yes, I think so.

And he would follow you anywhere?

Um. I think so.

~~Sad~~ God doesn't say anything for a long time/so I try to cheer her up

Lay it on me Sweet Lord!/The girl can take it!/Tell me what to do!

She says:All right, Evangeline.

Run

Run for your life

VI.
Every Creeping Thing That Creeps

Thousands of white angels glided past him as he traveled towards a great light ahead. He felt his eyes gently
blur open; yes, he was surrounded by angels, he was sure of
it, countless droves of them swirling at a distance in some
silent waltz, silver wings sparkling as they turned circles
in the warm glow. They were all dancing just for him. The
angels made no sound as they floated through the alabaster
fog; he could hear nothing except a faint ringing, like the
echo of a church bell. There were no angelic trumpets or
cheers or triumphant hymns to announce his passage into
Heaven. He *must* have died a hero, a soul deemed worthy
of such a welcoming parade of endless rows of angels, lighting his path. Slowly, his clouded vision began to sharpen as
the warm light became brighter. The toll of that bell grew
louder, now a steady hum in his ears. Did he even have ears
now? All he could see was white. So many nights of his life

had been spent dreaming of just this moment. But clearly this was no dream.

This was the end. He could feel it.

He could not move his body. He couldn't feel anything: his arms, his legs, his sore back. All he could see were the dancing angels, suspended around him in a muted procession.

Finally, Ben Wolf said to himself. *Thank you, God. Thank you. Thank you.*

He had waited so long for this moment; two lifetimes, in fact, if everything after the War counted as a second life. His first emotion was relief: *Oh my God, it was all true.* His faith had been rewarded just the way he had always dreamed, the way he had been told since he was a schoolboy: when you die, there will be a great, white light. There will be hosts of angels to guide you along the way. And when you reach Heaven, if you have lived a life worth living, all those you once loved will be standing there at the gates, waiting for you. When you die, all the sacrifices you made will be worth it. All your sins will be forgiven, all your questions will find answers.

When you die, your real life will begin.

As the white glow seeped closer and engulfed him, he could almost see her waiting for him, just ahead. He could even smell the familiar smoky musk of her favorite perfume. She was there, waiting for him. He felt his arm reaching for the light, but the intense pain from lifting it surprised him and made him recoil. Pain in heaven? Suddenly, a lonely trumpet broke the silence. It played a slow and sad melody, not the triumphant clarion call he'd expect for a hero's welcome. The pain spread to his head, forcing him to shutter his eyes for a moment in a wince. As he opened his eyes again, there was a voice.

"Wake up, Ben," it called to him. "Wake up."

I am awake, he thought. *I've never been so awake as right now.* He tried to concentrate on the angels dancing around him, but the light had become too bright, bleaching his eyesight as if he was snow-blind. *I am awake*, he repeated. But the angels began to melt into the white, like unexposed film put in sunlight.

"No, you ain't," the voice replied. "You need to wake up." The somber trumpet started again, and as his eyes focused and adjusted to the light, Ben began to cry; it was not the melancholy song that brought tears. Now he realized exactly where he was; there were no angels passing him, only snowflakes, drifting down from the white sky as he lay face-up on the cold ground. He was merely staring up at the white ceiling of clouds. He could feel the ache of his back pressed against a rock. The feeling in his arms was returning; his forehead throbbed like a bomb. As he sobbed, he could feel his own hands already on his face, covering his eyes welled up with tears. The skin on his cheeks stung with the frost. Slowly it sunk in that he was not in Heaven. Far from it; in fact, he had not traveled an inch. He knew the familiar feel of packed dirt in the compound of Armageddon. And he couldn't help but weep at the utter disappointment, the pain too much for an old, broken man.

"Now that ain't no way to act," the voice said. "Grown man, crying like that."

Ben tried to move his neck. As he shifted, everything on his body hurt at once, sending waves of pain up and down his spine like twisted spears poking under his skin.

Wait, he thought. *It was snowing? In Armageddon?* Suddenly he felt a rumble bubbling up from the pit of his stomach that turned the sobs into a wicked laughter. *Snow!* He hadn't seen a snowflake in more than thirty years now, so long ago he had forgotten what they looked like falling from the sky. He was laughing so hard his chest seared with pain every time he took a breath, but he couldn't stop.

"Well, that's better," the voice said, sounding closer now. "But what's so funny?"

"I thought the snowflakes were angels," Ben howled, still laughing like a child who had just played the perfect prank. "I thought the snow was angels, all waltzing around me."

"I don't even know how to waltz," the voice laughed along with him. "Sure sounds like one heck of a dream, though."

"But it *wasn't* a dream," Ben said sharply. "I know it wasn't."

"Whatever you say. You're the hero," the voice said. "One thing's for darn sure, though. You're sure lucky to be alive." Ben didn't recognize the voice, but it spoke to him as if they were old friends, or even old shipmates. And how did the voice know his name?

"I sure don't feel lucky," Ben replied as lay there, taking

stock of his limbs, his teeth, his vital organs. An old sailor's habit. His heart was pumping, that much was for sure. His body felt liked it'd been kicked by the mule a few hundred times, but at least everything still seemed to be in the right place. But suddenly his memory began to flood back, and the laughter abruptly ended. His instinct was to jump up, but when he tried to rise the pain was too much and he settled back down into the frozen ground. He tried to remember what happened before he had blacked out.

As his memory came back, he felt a heavy sense of dread. He had so many questions. Why didn't he hear any other voices? Why was there the strong smell of smoke in the air?

And where the hell did this snow come from? The boy hadn't even seen snow before—

The boy. His dull sense of dread sharpened to panic: where was the boy, and the girl? Suddenly he was frightened to sit up and see what was left of Armageddon but Ben managed to hoist himself up, grimacing with intense pain.

In front of him, Armageddon was in ruins. Underneath a thin blanket of snow, everything had been scorched black. The outbuildings were only blackened tatters of wood now, the barn reduced to a few stumps and wisps of grey smoke. Even the old railroad cars that had been stacked as an outer wall had been ripped apart like shreds of tin foil. There was nothing moving in front of him; all the animal pens were torched and empty but he could pick up the smell of charred flesh, a much darker scent that he unfortunately knew well. "Where's the boy?"

"He's fine," the voice said from behind him. "Right now he's over in Hyatt's workshop, or what's left of it. Trying to see if the truck is still going to work."

"And the girl," Ben said.

"She's gone," the voice said. "That snake snatched her up and flew back towards the mountains."

"Snake," Ben said. "You mean *dragon*."

"Snake, serpent, dragon, it's all the same to me. Tomato, to-mah-to, right? Trust me, I've seen it all, more than once." the voice said. "Now, you about ready?"

Ben nodded; he had been sitting long enough. He slowly got to his feet and turned around to finally see who was speaking. There was a man he'd never seen before sitting on the steps of Carnegie, which looked like a blackened molar now, wisps of grey smoke licking out of the empty doorways and windows into the cold air. The place was smoldering, the fires long since died out. He figured he must have been out for days.

"Where's everyone else?" There was an eerie quiet.

"Well, you want the nice version, or the true version?"

"I want the truth."

"Okay, then. They left you," he said. "Set out for the sea. Took what they could. Left you and the boy here without much thought. Hyatt's dead, but you knew that already. I guess I wasn't much surprised, though. No honor among thieves, isn't that what they used to say?"

Ben felt his blood heating up. "Just who the hell are you, mister?"

"Name's Gabriel," he said, tipping his hat. "Some folks call me Jib."

"Let me guess: you're another one just passing through." He remembered the stranger on the motorcycle from before. "We had another tourist come through. Old friend of yours?"

"Him? No way," Jib said. "Old enemy is a better way to put it."

"Well, that's a relief," Ben scoffed. "We got an old man, a boy and a trumpet player to fight a fucking dragon. Yeah, I like those odds."

The dragon had come again without warning, like a sudden storm. Ben could remember walking towards Carnegie and turning to look at the midday sky; a shadow grew around him on the ground. He looked up and in an instant had to dive to the ground, as a crooked claw the size of a dumptruck swooped down upon him, its fingers so close to his head he could see the empty spaces between its scales. He remembered springing up from pure instinct, slipping his rifle off his back and fumbling for the safety as he watched the great winged thing twist in the air, turning faster than he'd ever thought possible, heading straight for him for another run. In only a few more seconds, it was on him again.

It was all he could do to get a few rounds off before the world went black.

Then, the hosts of white angels.

Ben rubbed his throbbing forehead. "How long have I been out?"

"Too long," Jib said, pushing himself up from the steps and dusting off his trousers. "We've got some work to do. Finally time for you to be the hero."

Ben's pride was hurt. "What do you mean, *finally*?"

Gabriel spit. "Listen: do you think you're still alive by accident? Now, go find the boy."

Adam was digging through the charred wreckage of Hyatt's collapsed barn, putting every bit of his slight weight behind the splintered beams to push them aside. It was slow work. Ben watched from a distance; the boy seemed to have grown since the last time he'd seen him. Maybe not much taller or wider, Ben thought, but something about the kid definitely looked *older*. Maybe it was the way he stood: more like a man now, his shoulders squared as he worked the heavy beams. The snow had draped a thick white shroud over everything; every so often the boy would stop and swipe his hand through some of it, as if all this snow could be some mirage, a trick of the light. He scooped some to his nose, sniffing at it curiously.

"It's called snow," Ben said, coming closer. "Just frozen water, really."

"I knew that," the boy said, surprised someone had been watching. He dropped the white clump in his hand to the ground and wiped his palms together. The cold air was even stranger than the sight of snow, making him shudder. He had only known the hot desert until yesterday. "I have observed many pictures of snowflakes in the books of Carnegie."

There were pictures of children always smiling and playing as if they were holding spun sugar in their hands, as they made snow angels and fat snowmen. When he first touched the snow, he had expected the consistency of a cloud.

Adam turned to glance over at the charred husk that was once the library, and his home. "I wish we still had all the books of Carnegie," the boy said, looking at the hollow ruin that used to be his home. "They could state how to defeat a dragon."

Ben was about to tell the kid that all the monsters and boogeymen in those storybooks weren't real, just imaginary creations to scare children—but then he realized he'd just got his own ass kicked by a dragon. The rules were different now. Ben stepped through the splintered timbers and started pushing them aside, helping the boy. "I think the truck's going to be over there, under that pile," he said. "I've got to find something else we'll need over here."

The boy nodded and went back to work. "I have it. We can do what Siegfried did, when a dragon terrorized his hometown."

Ben would have laughed, if it didn't hurt so damned much. "Oh, yeah? What did old Siegfried do, Kid? Call in an airstrike?"

The boy's eyes stayed sharp and serious. "No. He dug a huge trench in the ground and hid inside it, until the dragon Fafnir passed over. Then he stabbed the dragon in the stomach with a magic sword and filled the trenches with blood. Then the dragon died."

"Well, amigo—I hate to be a downer, but we're short one magic sword," Ben said. "And one backhoe. Right now, we don't even have a gun that works. But we could ask the guy with the trumpet over there. After all, he seems to know everything we don't."

Adam looked at the demolished compound that surrounded them. "But there is only you and I here," the boy said. "Everyone else abandoned us. They believed you were killed by the dragon. And Hyatt has already gone to Disneyland."

Ben looked around for the trumpet player, but there was no sign of him now. "So you didn't see Gabriel? A man with a seersucker suit and polished shoes, over by Carnegie?"

The boy scratched his hair. "What is a seersucker?"

"Forget it." Under a jagged scrap of the tin roof, Ben had located what was left of Hyatt's work bench, and he crawled underneath it, a boy peeking in a cave, extending his hand to feel the floor in the darkness. "Here it is," he said, pulling out a small metal box and dusting it off. It was the plastic explosives Hyatt had somehow managed to make. A wizard, indeed. "Almost as good as a magic sword, right? I figure it worked for me on one monster, might as well try it again."

Adam folded his arms. "That is not how we will defeat the dragon."

"You sound pretty sure about that, Kid."

"I am sure. I talked to God. He told me."

Ben's mouth fell open. "God told you,"

The boy sounded confused. "Yes. You do not talk to God?"

"Usually it's a one-sided conversation, Kid. You talk to Him often?"

"Every day. Evangeline does, too."

Ben rubbed his forehead. He wasn't quite sure he wasn't still in some crazy dream. One thing was for certain: he wished he could talk to God, right now. He felt like giving the man upstairs a piece of his mind.

The boy kept his arms folded, peering at the old man with unsure eyes. "So, do you want to know how it ends?"

"How *what* ends, kid? Are you telling me you know what's going to happen next, tomorrow, the next day?"

"That is correct."

Ben pointed towards the mountain, which was white with snow now. "So you already know if I die up there, or not?"

"You mean when *we* leave. So do you want to know?" Who was this kid standing here? It seemed like a completely different version than the one engulfed in books, writing lists all day. Did he really know everything that was going to happen? Who was following who now?

"No," Ben said, thinking about it. "No, I don't want to know."

Adam turned, and went back to uncovering the truck. "You would not leave me behind tomorrow, would you?"

Somehow, Ben managed to crack a smile. "Kid, I was about to ask you the same thing."

Eve woke up in almost total darkness. As her eyes adjusted to the dim she noticed a single prick of light, far in the distance. Her hands felt around her. There was just enough light for her to realize she was on the floor of some huge cavern, the ceiling too far to see. The floor was made of smooth, dark stones. As her eyes adjusted, she guessed the faint white glow came from a passage that led off somewhere. Or nowhere, she thought.

"Hello?" she called out, but there was no answer, only the hollow echo of her own voice rolling back at her. How did she end up here? The last thing she remembered, she was *flying*—held tightly in one of the dragon's massive claws, watching the brown desert roll by beneath her. She remembered crying at first but moments of wonder had also found a way to seep in—after all, she was *flying*, thousands of feet in the air. The first person to fly, like the birds. The serpent's talons had held her firmly as they swooped west towards the mountains.

The *mountains*, she thought. That had to be where she was right now, somewhere deep inside Mount Megiddo. Inside the cave it was oddly cold; she brought her knees up to her chin to keep from shivering as she waited in the darkness. How long had she been in here? Her stomach rumbled with hunger.

Adam would come for her, she was sure of it. God had said he would.

God hadn't mentioned anything about being kidnapped by a dragon, though.

Eve couldn't see much of her own body, only shadows—but she did not feel sore, or injured. She felt restless more than anything; there must be a dragon around here someplace, she thought. It was probably a good idea to start looking for the exit. Getting up and walking might warm her up a little, too.

"Hello?" she called out again, feeling a pang of despair grow in her throat.

This time, she could hear a voice in the distance. "Where are you, my child?" It was a familiar voice, and it sounded like it was coming from the direction of the faint white light. But with the echo, she couldn't be sure.

Eve sprang to her feet and dusted herself off, excited. "Is that you, God?"

"What are you doing sitting in the dark, girl?" Then there was a hearty laugh that almost sounded like a roar as it bounced off the rock walls. "You belong out here, in the light. You belong with me."

"Where are you, Sweet Lord?" Eve stepped towards the light ahead, feeling the way ahead with her bare feet. "Is Adam there with you?"

"He'll be along," the voice said. "Don't you worry, girl. Come now. I have so much to show you."

Slowly, Eve took another step towards the light, then another. Adam would come looking for her, she could feel it. It felt strange being apart from him, they had been together so long. She had only been awake in this cave for a few minutes, and so far she'd stopped herself at least twice before she asked Adam what they should do now, even though he wasn't here.

She laughed to herself; for once, she'd be happy to see one of his maps.

She crept slowly in the direction of the light. As she got closer, she realized it was coming from the end of a smaller cavern, a passageway that snaked away from the huge circular cave she found herself in now. Now she could make out countless other passages leading in other direction from the cavern like a maze, all of them completely dark.

"That's it," the voice called to her from the lighted passage. "This way. That's my girl."

Eve stood at the rim of the twisted passageway, turning her head around for a moment to search the darkness she was leaving behind. What if Adam was trying to find her? How would he know which way to go? She wanted to leave Adam a sign; she'd write him a note if she still had her book, but there was nothing.

She ran her hand along the smooth rock of the wall and suddenly it came to her: she bent down and felt for one of the jagged, loose rocks that lay at her feet. When she found one about the size of her palm she stood back up and scraped it against the wall; in the dim light she saw it left a chalky mark. Perfect, she thought. Now all she had to do is think of what to draw: something only Adam would know.

It only took her a second. She laughed when she pictured Adam finding it. She went to work in the dull light, still laughing a little to herself as the mark took shape, holding her flat rock like a knife and rasping it hard against the rough wall. She could feel her knuckles getting raw.

Finally, she took a step back from the wall to look at her handiwork, and nodded approval. *That should do it*, she muttered to herself.

"Are you coming, child?" This time, the voice sounded a bit impatient.

"I'm coming, Sweet Lord," Eve called out, dropping the rock to the floor. "Here I come."

The truck's engine roared to life on the first turn. Ben and the boy had packed the truck bed with anything useful they could find: scraps of food, a coil of rope, and wrapped inside a pile of blankets, the metal box of semtex and detonators Hyatt had left behind. There were no working rifles left; Ben's had been mangled like art and the others must have taken the rest, along with any ammunition.

Guns probably wouldn't do much anyway, Ben thought to himself.

The old man kneeled down next to the truck to check the tires, look at the axles. He rapped his fist against the belly of the gas tank. "Probably got enough fuel to make it to the mountain," Ben called to the boy, who was busy tying down their load in the bed. "But probably not enough to make it back."

The boy shrugged his shoulders. "I know I am not coming back."

Ben stood up and stared at the boy. "What's that supposed to mean, Kid?"

The boy shrugged again. "I know I am not returning from the mountain."

Ben shook his head. "Because God told you."

"Yes, because God told me. And my name is *Adam* now, not Kid. Kid is not a proper name." Adam finished working the last knot and tested the tautness of the rope. It was hard to tell who was the old man in this conversation, and who was the child. It confused Ben even more that the boy's bushy hair was now crusted white, tinted with snowflakes.

Adam climbed down from the truck. "Do *you* want to know if you are coming back?"

"I think I already know the answer to that," Ben replied. "No word from God necessary."

It was getting colder by the hour, and the snow did not show any signs of relenting. There must have been close to a foot already on the ground. Ben found the dog's old blanket hidden beneath the snow and ripped it into two jagged halves with his knife, slitting a hole in the middle of each half. He slipped one over the boy's head, a makeshift poncho to protect his slender bones from the cold. When the boy tied a length of rope around his thin waist, instantly the outfit reminded Ben of a character from some old drama: a squire or page for some medieval knight. Ben put on the other half and realized they were matching now. *I hope dragons are scared of color coordination,* he muttered to himself. He felt warmer, anyway. Ben took one last turn around Armageddon before they headed out for good. He lingered at the steps of the old library, peering inside the ruined doorway as if waiting for someone to come out. But there was no one left, just him and the boy, and hopefully, the girl. Blowing snow had started to cover the inside of the gutted building, but he could still smell the ashes of all those dead books in the basement. For some strange reason he was in a good mood, almost happy, even though he knew he was never coming back here.

The boy wanted to drive. Ben couldn't see anything wrong with it, especially because there was nothing to run into in the flatness between Armageddon and the base of the mountain. At least, he hoped there wasn't. And it didn't seem right denying a boy his God-given right to drive a pickup through the snow. Ben climbed into the passenger seat and watched the boy fumble with the pedals and gearshift. The truck started to roll, slowly. The boy steered them through the ruined gate of Armageddon and out into the new, white wilderness. Ben bit his lip as they grinded along in first gear for at least the first mile, cruising at five miles per hour. The boy was gripping the steering wheel like he was wrestling a grizzly bear with both hands.

"Press down harder on the clutch," Ben yelled over the noise of the engine. "Try second gear."

"I can *do* it," Adam shouted back, breathing hard. His skinny legs were stretched all the way to floor. "This is a lot harder than I thought."

"You're doing fine. Besides, most kids never learned to drive in an armored car." Ben tried to wipe some frost from the windshield with his forearm. "And I guess it was a lot easier when there were actual roads."

Adam found third gear and the truck lurched ahead faster now. He was checking his mirrors, even though the truck had no mirrors. "In the old world, did you drive a pickup truck?"

"I sure did," Ben said, smiling as the dusty memory tumbled down to him. "It was my dad's before he gave it to me. Lot like this one, actually—before Hyatt turned it into the Incredible Hulk. Took my driving test in it, failed miserably."

"You had to pass a test to drive pickup trucks in Texas?"

"Oh, sure," Ben said. "Everyone did. Cars, motorcycles. I can give you the test right now, if you like."

The boy beamed a wide smile. "I would like that very much."

"Okay," Ben said, shifting in his seat and putting his hands out. "Tell you what, we'll skip the parallel parking. If you get us to the foot of that mountain alive, you pass with flying colors. Deal?"

"It is a deal," Adam said. Fresh snow was piling up on the hood. Some of it was blowing in through the louvers, covering the dash with drifts of white dust. "I cannot see through the front anymore."

"A windshield would help, huh? Yeah, maybe a heater, too. Stop the truck a minute, I'll get out and clean the snow off the hood for you." The kid nodded and jammed his toes on the brake too quickly, the truck sliding to an abrupt halt. Ben had to brace himself against the dash to prevent his forehead from smacking against the grill. He let out a low whistle. "Well, Adam, you pass the *sudden stop* part of the test with flying colors."

The boy beamed another smile. "To be honesty?"

"You bet. You just saved that lady pushing her baby carriage across the parking lot." Ben cranked open his door and slid off his seat, bracing himself for the wind. His feet crunched in the deep snow. It felt colder out here than before. The sky seemed darker, too.

Adam yelled out to him. "I do not observe any old ladies anywhere."

"Keep looking, Adam. She's out there." Ben leaned over the front of the truck and used his arms to plow some of the snow off the hood. There was nothing on the horizon but shades of white and grey, no landmarks but the mountains looming in the distance. Every time his eyes caught the sight of Mount Megiddo in the distance, his mood soured instantly; a second before, he found himself in a good mood, having fun with the Kid and his first driving lesson. But the mountain reminded him instantly of where they were going, and what they had to do.

Suddenly Ben felt something hit the side of his face, knocking him out of his daydream. "What the—" His cheek stung as he swiveled around, reaching for his knife out of instinct, ready for an attack.

The boy stood on the other side of the truck, doubled over from laughing. Ben felt his red cheek and realized he'd been the target of the boy's first snowball.

"You should have observed your face," the boy said, pointing at him over the hood.

"The Astros could have used you on the mound," Ben said, rubbing his sore face. The boy did not stop laughing. Ben turned to look at the mountain again. "This isn't one of your storybooks from the library, you know."

"But you are wrong," Adam said. "This is exactly like the stories from Carnegie. There is a hero, and a villain. Are you sure you do not want to know how it ends?"

"You know what, Nostradamus, if you know everything, tell me if I get to go to Heaven by the end of your story. Tell me if God mentioned that."

"I do not know that. I do know that Eve and I cannot finish the story without your help."

Ben shook the snow off his arms and went back to the truck. "Well, I guess it's nice to be needed."

"Of course you are needed, you are the hero of the story." Adam climbed in and searched for a gear.

Ben slumped back in his seat. "I'll just have to wait for the miniseries to come out, then."

"What is a miniseries?"

"Just another kind of story, I guess. You had to tune in every week to watch."

"Did it have heroes and villains?"

"Oh, yeah. Lots of them. Maybe even a few damsels in distress."

"*Damsel* is an old English word for girl."

"Bingo. Speaking of which, let's try for second gear this

time, buddy. We've got a date."

The boy wrestled with the truck until he found it. "Can I ask you one more question?"

"Sure, Kid—I mean, *Adam*. Shoot."

"What is a Nostradamus?"

Mount Megiddo seemed a lot steeper than Ben remembered. The thick snowfall had erased any landmarks and made his footing on the flat rocks slippery. Even with the snow covering the face of the mountain, this part felt very familiar to him for a reason he couldn't quite place. Ben found a flat stretch beneath an outcropping of rock and dropped his pack to the ground, bending forward to his knees, trying to catch his shallow breath. They were probably about halfway up the east face now. Ben could only see a sea of white below; even the truck, which had become a black dot at the base of the mountain, had disappeared from view, covered in the heavy snow. They could not tell if it was day or night anymore; there was no dark or light to the world anymore, everything bathed in a dull grey. The sun and moon were only memories now, both completely hidden behind an impenetrable wall of clouds. Adam had gone up ahead, picking his way between the boulders that littered the slope, but he turned back when he saw Ben was no longer following his trail.

Adam called to him from above, his voice echoing down the mountainside. "Why are you stopping?"

"You look tired," Ben lied to him, his hands cupped

around his mouth. "We'll camp here, make it to the top in the morning." He pointed to the closest steam vent, a few dozen yards to his left; with the squared boulder crouched beside it, they could sling their blankets down from one side with ropes and make a decent shelter from the storm, the hot steam from the vent protecting them from the bitter cold. Even though it was covered in white, this boulder seemed so familiar to Ben, but he could not place why. His frosted breath wheezed in and out of his ruined lungs.

The boy gave him a quizzical look in return. "I do not feel very tired."

Ben was still gasping hard. "Trust me. We'll rest here, and get a fresh start in a few hours."

It was an old man's lie. Ben was the one who had suddenly grown tired, struggling just to make it this far. The hemp bag strapped to his back had felt like an anchor, dragging him down to the ground with every step. He didn't want the kid to know it, but he felt so weak, like his bones were suddenly hollow, or made of powder. This was more than simple age or weariness or lack of sleep. It was something different; right now, he felt like an hourglass with the bottom seal taken out, the sand tumbling out. Soon he'd be empty. The closer he got to the top of this mountain, it seemed the weaker he got. Tomorrow, he might have to crawl the last few hundred yards to the top. If he made it to tomorrow. His legs had begun to feel numb. He didn't want to alarm the boy. Maybe a couple hours of sleep would change things.

They both huddled under their makeshift tent and ate the last of their food. Adam would look at him after each bite, looking the old man over with a sharp eye. "I can carry Hyatt's box if you are too tired to carry it."

"Nonsense," Ben said, his back stiffening. "This is my fight, too, you know."

"I am not positive there must be a fight. I know I am supposed to find the girl."

Ben rubbed his hands in the hot vapor that issued from the steam vent between them, trying to keep them warm. "Do you miss her?"

"I do not miss her," the boy replied immediately, like any other reflex.

"It's okay to miss someone," Ben said, fighting to stay awake. God, he was so tired now. "She probably misses you, too. We'll find her tomorrow for sure, don't worry."

"But I am *not* worried, because I know I will see her again."

"Oh, I forgot," Ben said, rolling his sleepy eyes as he turned over on his side. "You already know how this whole thing ends."

"This is correct." The boy looked over at him, studying the old man who had been his hero for so long. "Do you want to know –"

"Damn it, the answer's still no," Ben said harshly, cutting him off. "Anyway, I got a pretty good idea now."

The boy perked up. "Has God spoken to you, as well?"

Ben tried to rub his numb leg. "Oh, he's talking, all right."

Adam scratched at his temple. "If you do not talk with God, how do you know what to do? How do you know anything at all?"

"Now *that*," Ben said, "is one question I can't answer. It used to be called *faith*. Not sure what to call it now, in this crazy fucked-up world we're in. Maybe stupidity? Or hell, just *suicide*. Whatever it is, I'm not sure I have it anymore. You're different, Adam. You and the girl. You two are part of a new world, and I'm part of an old one."

As Adam listened, he drew his legs up to his stomach, leaning on his side and pulling a blanket to his chin. He rocked back and forth in that position, biting his lip, obviously thinking hard about something. For a brief moment, he seemed more like a kid again. His eyes drooped with sleep. "In Texas, people did not talk to God?"

"I guess they did, in a way. But only when they needed something," Ben said. He took in a shallow breath. "Or when they were sure they were about to die." He lay back now too, drowsy and strangely calm. He wondered if he closed his eyes right now if he would ever wake up, he was that tired. He watched as the boy twitched beside him, already deep into some dream. He believed Adam could speak with God. Ben felt a stab of jealousy: right now, he wanted to talk to God more than anything. He thought he'd earned that chance by now. Being left behind on what was left of the world had always seemed like punishment enough, for whatever he had done wrong.

He watched the snow continue to fall outside their

makeshift lean-to. Ben suddenly realized why this part of the mountain felt so familiar: this was exactly where he had found the boy, years ago. The memory of that day was still clear in his mind: he had spent a long, sun-baked afternoon helping Hyatt search for minerals among the rocks at the foot of the mountain, when he heard a child crying somewhere above him. He was sure it was the wind, or worse, one of the monsters that lingered in the desert surrounding Armageddon. But when he approached the square-shaped boulder from below, he could first see the wild hair of the boy, blowing in the hot wind like a tumbleweed. As he got closer, he saw the explosion of hair was indeed attached to a naked boy. There was a look of shock on his small face, eyes wide as if this was his very first glance at the new world around him.

"Why am I even here," he mumbled to himself, half-asleep. "You two don't need me."

"We do need you." The boy's alert voice surprised him, as if he had been awake the whole time. "You are the hero."

That's the last thing Ben felt like now.

In the dark, the boy sounded like he had begun to cry.

Ben tried to sit up, but couldn't find the strength. "Are you crying?"

"You do not know how your story ends," the boy said, wiping away tears from his face. "I am sad, because I do."

There was a white glow emanating up ahead. As the cavern narrowed even more, Eve looked back into the darkness. The air was so much warmer now, almost *steamy*, and she could feel her skin starting to bead with sweat. Absentmindedly, she dropped the rock she'd carried from the cave, and it clattered noisily to the floor, making her crouch. *Nice work, Evangeline*, she cursed to herself. *Why don't you blow a damn trumpet next time, girl.* She listened for anything moving in the corridor behind her, but there was only a still silence. Quietly, she slinked towards the light ahead, every so often stealing a look behind her. After a sharp bend the passage had shrunk to the size of a small hallway now, the white light bright in her eyes now and directly ahead, glinting off the smooth rock face of the cave walls like glass. Now the air was so hot she could feel the vapor sitting in her lungs, making it harder to breathe.

Eve continued down the passage until she could make out the end, about a hundred feet in front of her. Standing there, she swore she could hear the faint echo of voices in the distance—not human voices but a cacophony of what seemed like every other language she knew: turtle, owl, coyote, iguana, prairie dog. They were all mixed together, issuing down the corridor as a wall of white noise. As she crept closer to the light, she became excited when she recognized individual voices: the song of fish, and the constant chatter of crows. Some of them were new voices she had never heard, living in Alabama or Armageddon. The voices all sounded so happy as they babbled on top of one another; Eve couldn't help but smile. Dappled sunlight filtered through the mist ahead, covering what looked like a world of green—wait, were those trees?

Adam was going to faint on the spot when he saw all these green, glorious trees.

"Come out into the light," the voice called out to her as she hugged the wall of the cave. "That's it, child. Come out where I can see you."

Eve stepped backwards a half-step, her shoulder blades hugging the wall of the cave. She couldn't see God anywhere, but the voice was warm and friendly. Still, Eve kept her distance. "Is that you, Lord?"

"Come into the light, my sweet girl," the voice called again. "There is so much for you to see." Eve didn't exactly know why, but the voice sounded both familiar and strange at the same time.

"Maybe I should wait for Adam," Eve said. "He should be here soon."

"Oh, my sweet child," the voice said, laughing. "Since when are you the kind of girl who waits?"

That made Eve crack a smile. "I'm coming, Lord," she said, edging her feet forward along the cave floor, as if she was walking a trapeze. She took another tentative step forward, then another. She could make out the trees now, millions of them below her shrouded in white mist, all bristling with dew. For the first time she could smell the damp earth and warm buds that must be bursting below. Beyond the lush green forest she could see green meadows stretching as far as her eyes could see.

She already had a million questions. Why was the sky blue here, on this side of the mountain? She glanced behind her into the black cave, thinking of Adam, already looking forward to exploring all of this together with him. Eve inched forward towards the light, feeling the excitement churn in her stomach. The sunlight ahead seemed to warm her bones. Only a couple more steps now, and she would be totally immersed in the light.

"That's my girl," the voice said. "We will have so much fun here, you'll see."

Eve stopped and bit her lip, lifting her hand to shield her eyes from the harsh sunlight ahead. "It *is* you, isn't it, Lord?"

"Just you come with me," the voice said. "I have so much to tell you."

When Ben woke up in their makeshift tent, the boy was gone. He struggled to sit up and look around; it was still snowing heavily outside. "Adam?" he called out, trying to scramble to his feet. His legs were heavy. "Are you there?" There was no answer. The boy had left him behind. Or worse, something had taken him. Ben quickly reached for his pack: it was still there, but it had been opened, the top flap hanging loose.

The explosives were gone, too.

It took all his strength just to rise to his feet, but he did it, stumbling head first out into the cold, the world completely white now, everything covered with deep snow as the frozen wind whipped around him. He found the boy's fresh tracks in the snow, snaking up around the square boulder towards the summit. "*Adam*," he shouted again, but he could not see the boy anywhere ahead.

Why did he leave me behind, so close to the top?

"He thought he could save you," a voice called from above. It was the trumpet player, sitting on the boulder, unfazed by the weather as he looked down at him with a pitying gaze. He was clicking his tongue. "That boy's in trouble," Jib said. "He needs your help, one last time."

"I can't," Ben said. "I can barely walk. I'm so *tired*."

"Let me get this straight. You always want to know why you got left behind, all those years ago, right?" He turned his head to look up the mountainside, at the trail the boy had left behind. "And you're telling me you don't know by now?"

Adam peered in the dark cavern. He held a candle lantern in front of him as he walked. The cave he had found at the top of the mountain had led him here, a huge opening with what looked like a hundred smaller passageways leading off into the darkness. He was glad to be out of the snow, although it wasn't much warmer in here.

"Evangeline?" he called out, his voice echoing across the empty space. "Eve?"

He started to process the math in his head about the chances he would choose the right way out, the passage that would lead him to her. He stopped when the number grew to the millions. He felt his way along the curved wall of the cave, peering down each dark hallway with growing despair.

He must have passed a hundred passages, all looking exactly the same, until the dim light from his lantern caught something etched into the wall:

The boy smiled. This was the way, no doubt. He took a step inside; was that a pinpoint of white light, coming from the other end?

"Adam?" It was Ben's voice coming from the darkness behind him. The old man must have followed him. "Adam, are you there?"

The boy turned back and found Ben hugging the wall in the darkness. He looked like he was about to collapse against the rock wall. His bloodshot eyes were wide with fear. Adam ran to him and dropped his pack to the floor, looking for his jug inside to offer the old hero a drink of water. But Ben pushed the jug away, trying to catch his breath. "Tell me, kid, you still got that box of Hyatt's?"

Adam nodded. "It's here, in my pack."

"Good," the old man wheezed. "Get it out. *Quick.*"

"There is no need," the boy assured him softly. "I have found Eve. She is near."

Ben clutched the boy's shirt and pulled their faces together. "Listen, there *is* a fucking need, and it's coming right behind me." The old man wrestled with the hinge to the metal box. Adam had never seen his hero so much in panic before, so scared of something.

Suddenly there was a terrible roar that shook the rocks under their feet, like an earthquake. Adam looked down the wide passage to see two huge eyes, the color of a sunset smoldering deep in the darkness.

"Go to her," Ben said, pushing the boy the other way. "Run!"

Adam raced forward a few steps, then stopped. "Are you coming?"

Ben sagged against the wall, fumbling with the box. "And I thought you already knew how this story ends."

Solemnly, the boy nodded.

Ben held his hand up in the air and waved it back and forth. "Remember, this is how people in Texas used to say goodbye."

Adam waved back until the old hero turned away, the open box of explosives cradled in his arms like a baby.

Ben turned back to face the two sinister eyes looming in the blackness. There was no time to hook up a timer to the slapper detonator, he thought; besides, he felt so weak now he doubted he could throw anything very far.

No, there was only one solution: he would deliver this one himself, in person.

As he walked forward, banging off each side of the cavern in the dark, his thumb found the pressure pad on the slapper and he jabbed the prong end into one of the semtex packs. All he would have to do now is squeeze his hand together hard, and this cavern would instantly become a tomb. He turned his head back to the light one more time; the boy had disappeared around the bend.

"We meet again," he called out into the darkness. He looked back one more time; the boy's lantern had disappeared behind him.

There was another roar, a blast of hot sulphur rushing past Ben's face like a foul wind. He gripped the box tightly and trudged forward a few more steps. "Got something for you, my friend." He tried to break into a run, limping badly as he felt for the cavern walls with his free hand, the open box tucked under his arm like he was carrying a football. He bounced off one wall but kept going, struggling to stay upright. He couldn't feel his legs anymore. He couldn't feel much of anything now.

This was the end. He could feel it.

VII.
You Shall Eat Dust All the Days of Your Life

Hush now, my child. Hush now, my sweet, sweet girl. Do not cry. Let me whisper in your ear all the secrets you deserve to know. Why are you so frightened? I am not the monster; I am your friend. Come closer and touch my coils: don't you see? My scales are soft to the touch. Listen to my voice: what do you hear? There is no thunderous roar or sinister hiss, just a gentle song. Forget what you were taught about good and evil. Would a monster defend you while you sleep, or shield you from the hot sun with his wings? Would a demon sing you such a sweet lullaby? No, my angel, I am not the villain. A villain is a wrathful God who tells you exactly what to eat and where to go. A villain orders a poet to stop being curious. Only something evil would force a girl to stop being herself.

Why love God, when She asks you to live your whole life as both a poet and a slave?

In your heart, you know a poet must write whatever feels important. You believe a girl should be able to eat anything she wants! Look at that tree behind you, sitting alone in the middle of that perfect green meadow; have you ever seen such beautiful fruit? Here, I will pluck one from the highest branch, just for you. In fact, I will pluck two, and place them in your lap for later, so that you and Adam may eat together, when he comes. He will be here soon to find you, and he will surely be hungry. Share this lovely fruit, and surely he will love you forever.

I am not the monster, my love. The only monster here is the one who keeps so many secrets to Herself.

Come closer, and I will tell you all the secrets of the world.

Here is the first one: all of this is yours.

Hush now, my darling. Sleep now, my beautiful girl. Do not be afraid. Keep still, and listen to my lullaby. Let me cradle you in my soft talons and sing for you. Let my coils surround you and protect you from all that is wild in this newborn, hungry world. I will watch over you while you rest, and I will cool your skin with a breeze from my wings as I tell you a story.

Hush now, Sleep now, and dream of the days ahead. Here he comes now. Can you hear his footsteps in the distance? Can you hear his voice, calling out for you? I told you Adam will be here soon. He will listen to anything you say, because he loves you. The boy will eat anything you eat, and he will dream anything you dream. Together, you will have a heavy weight to bear. Thousands of years from now, people will still remember your name. All stories will begin with you. The poems and songs of every future generation will chant your name out loud. So sleep now, rest your weary head. You have come so far, and you have seen so much already.

Do not forsake me, my darling. When you awake, this whole world will be yours, and I will have to slither across it all the days of my life. Do not forget me, my sensational girl. For when you awake, you will be in love, and I will be alone. I will be the pariah, the one everyone hates. But you will be the Queen of Paradise. You will be able to name everything you see. So listen, my child. Listen to the story of one world ending, and another world ready to begin.

A Note About Beowulf

Like its titular character, *Beowulf* deftly evades efforts to get a firm grip on it. Consider the poem's last words, which refer to the fallen king as *lof-geornost*—"most eager for fame," as Howell Chickering's lucid translation puts it. The poem refuses to let us know exactly how we should respond to this aspect of Beowulf's character. Should we celebrate his zeal for renown, since it motivated him to protect his people and conquer terrifying opponents? Or should we regard it as the misguided aspiration of a man unable to apprehend higher spiritual truths?

Before making a judgment, it might be useful to reflect on Anglo-Saxon artistry in general. Recall the elaborately engraved sword-hilt Beowulf brings back to Hrothgar, and the *wunden gold* found in the dragon's lair. Take an online look at the intricately designed hilts and chest-pieces found in the Staffordshire Hoard, a trove of Anglo-Saxon treasures first unearthed in 2009. Artists in this culture decorated objects' surfaces in a manner that is anything but superficial. Twisted serpents and tangled symbols turn even the simplest tool into something both highly stylized and practically writhing with life.

With this in mind, we might want to think less about mastering *Beowulf* than about entangling ourselves in it.

The more we try to sort through Beowulf's motives in taking on the dragon single-handedly or to understand the quasi-human emotions of Grendel and his mother, the more we find ourselves encountering contradictory characteristics and unexpected turns of phrase in the poem. Getting tied up in interpretive knots is uncomfortable, of course. But perhaps this experience brings us closer to the Anglo-Saxons' world view, which seems to have encompassed salvific Christian truths, uncompromising warrior ideals, awed engagement with the natural world, and an inexhaustible delight in wordplay, among many other thoughts and emotions. Bravely embracing the poem's complexity might even make a little bit of Beowulf rub off on us. Like our *lofgeornost* hero, we become eager, restless, and superlative in our striving.

—*Moira Fitzgibbons, Ph.D.*

Tommy Zurhellen was born in New York City. With assistance from the GI Bill, he earned an MFA in Fiction at the University of Alabama in 2002 and since then his short fiction and essays have appeared in a variety of journals, including *Carolina Quarterly*, *Appalachee Review* and *Quarterly West*. *Armageddon, Texas* is the third and final book in the Messiah Trilogy, following *Nazareth, North Dakota* (2011) and *Apostle Islands* (2012), all from Atticus Books. Tommy currently teaches writing at Marist College in upstate New York. He is also co-host of the popular podcast Fiction School; you can find out more about Tommy and his writing projects at the Fiction School website, *www.fictionschool.com*.

Moira Fitzgibbons, Ph.D. (*A Note About Beowulf, Epigraph Translation*) is Associate Professor of English at Marist College, where she recites Old English poetry out loud whenever the occasion presents itself. She suggests that anyone who enjoys *Beowulf* should also check out the shorter poems, "The Seafarer" and "The Battle of Maldon."

A Note About the Characters
(To be read upon completion of *Armageddon, Texas*)

The story of *Armageddon, Texas* is a retelling of two ancient tales: the biblical account of *Genesis*, where a new world is created; and the medieval pagan poem *Beowulf*, where an old world passes away. Many of the characters found in *Armageddon, Texas* are inspired by people in these original narratives. Below are brief descriptions of select characters; the personality upon whom the character was loosely based is in parentheses.

Beowulf
In the medieval world depicted in the poem *Beowulf*, pagan gods are slowly being replaced by Christianity; belief in magic is being supplanted by faith in a new God. The poem is an account of the great deeds of Beowulf, the world's last hero. He slays the monster Grendel, then Grendel's mother, and finally at the end of his life, he defeats a fire-breathing dragon threatening his kingdom.

Ben Wolf (Beowulf) is this Earth's last hero. A man of faith before the apocalypse, he wonders why he had been left behind on a barren earth, when so many others have been taken to the afterlife before him. Not even he is sure why he is driven to perform good deeds in the face of so much chaos and destruction. He is known by others left behind as the man who hunted down the maniacal murderer

Frank Dayraven (Dayraven the Frank) in the Holy land, what used to be called North Dakota.

Ben's mentor and only friend is **Hyatt Lacy** (Hygelac) who qualifies as some sort of wizard in this broken world, with his knowledge of explosives. Unlike Ben, Hyatt understands why he was left behind: his prior life as a terrorist probably doomed him anyway. But even for a man as jaded as Hyatt Lacy, the promise of redemption can be a siren song.

Ben Wolf and his warriors travel across the Alabama Sea to rid a self-proclaimed king **Pike** (Hrothgar) of an otherworldly monster that has landed on the shores of Talladega for some unknown purpose. Pike's long suffering wife **Wilma** (Wealhtheow) sees something different in the strange hero who has come to Talladega; Pike's chief adviser **Worthy** (Unferth) is also suspicious of the newcomers' reasons for coming so far.

The monster that has terrorized the walled town is actually the bastard son of the Messiah, **Samson** (Grendel) who is journeying west towards Armageddon and the promise of paradise in the mountains. His mother, **Daylene Hooker** (Grendel's mother) is world-weary and bitter; she has even more reason than Ben to question why she is still here, instead of walking the golden avenues of paradise with her one love, Sam Davidson. But she is still a mother, and when her son is threatened, she turns to the only power she has left: revenge.

Long after this adventure, Ben's town of Armageddon is suddenly threatened by a fire-breathing dragon. In one last quest, he knows he must travel to Mount Megiddo and defeat the beast, to fulfill his destiny. Abandoned by the aging warriors who once stood firmly beside him, Ben must journey to the mountain with only **the Kid** (Wiglaf) beside him. After a lifetime of questions, Ben seems to finally understand his fate.

Genesis

The Book of Genesis begins with God creating Earth out of the void in seven days, including one day of rest. In the account, God gradually creates all living things to inhabit the Earth, but He is not satisfied until he creates Man in his own image. The first humans, Adam and Eve, have the great responsibility of taking care of the Garden, as well as naming all its creatures and plants. They have the power to talk with all animals. God's only rule for the first humans is to never eat from a certain tree, which the serpent recognizes as the Tree of Knowledge. But the serpent (widely recognized as a form of Satan) convinces Eve to eat from the tree, and to get Adam to eat the fruit as well. When God realizes their actions, he banishes Adam and Eve from paradise forever to a life of hardship, and curses the snake to crawl on his belly instead of walk upright.

Each of the chapter titles in *Armageddon, Texas* corresponds to a day of Creation, beginning with the Void and ending with God's warning to the serpent, "You will eat dust all the days of your life."

The Kid (Adam) is the only boy left on Earth, and he has no memory of the apocalypse or the world that came before it. He was found one day on the rocky slopes of Mount Megiddo by Ben Wolf and Hyatt Lacy. Since then, he has become curious about the history of this old world where Ben and Hyatt came from. He lives in the basement of the only firm structure in Armageddon, the former Carnegie library, where he is surrounded by books. His only companion is the dog named **Dog**, who also believes he is the only one of his kind left on the planet.

The Kid and Dog both must change their thinking when one day, Ben returns from an adventure with the girl **Evangeline** (Eve) who looks almost like the Kid's twin in appearance. However, appearance is about all they have in common; while the boy is all about order and learning the rules, the girl is dead-set on a life devoted to breaking the rules. Through all this, though, they inevitably become best friends.

The Dragon (Serpent) carries Eve away to the mountain, knowing that the new paradise is hidden on the other side; he figures if he can convince the girl, she will convince the boy that they should eat from the forbidden tree. Along with the hero Ben, Adam sets off on a journey to find Eve, and start their new life together at the beginning of a new world.